KILLER

THE CLASSIC HANK JANSON

The first original Hank Janson book appeared in 1946, and the last in 1971. However, the classic era on which we are focusing in the Telos reissue series lasted from 1946 to 1953. The following is a checklist of those books, which were subdivided into five main series and a number of 'specials'.

PRE-SERIES BOOKS
When Dames Get Tough (1946)
Scarred Faces (1947)

SERIES ONE
1) This Woman Is Death (1948)
2) Lady, Mind That Corpse (1948)
3) Gun Moll For Hire (1948)
4) No Regrets For Clara (194)
5) Smart Girls Don't Talk (1949)
6) Lilies For My Lovely (1949)
7) Blonde On The Spot (1949)
8) Honey, Take My Gun (1949)
9) Sweetheart, Here's Your Grave (1949)
10) Gunsmoke In Her Eyes (1949)
11) Angel, Shoot To Kill (1949)
12) Slay-Ride For Cutie (1949)

SERIES TWO
13) Sister, Don't Hate Me (1949)
14) Some Look Better Dead (1950)
15) Sweetie, Hold Me Tight (1950)
16) Torment For Trixie (1950)
17) Don't Dare Me, Sugar (1950)
18) The Lady Has A Scar (1950)
19) The Jane With The Green Eyes (1950)
20) Lola Brought Her Wreath (1950)
21) Lady, Toll The Bell (1950)
22) The Bride Wore Weeds (1950)
23) Don't Mourn Me Toots (1951)
24) This Dame Dies Soon (1951)

SERIES THREE
25) Baby, Don't Dare Squeal (1951)
26) Death Wore A Petticoat (1951)
27) Hotsy, You'll Be Chilled (1951)

28) It's Always Eve That Weeps (1951)
29) Frails Can Be So Tough (1951)
30) Milady Took The Rap (1951)
31) Women Hate Till Death (1951)
32) Broads Don't Scare Easy (1951)
33) Skirts Bring Me Sorrow (1951)
34) Sadie Don't Cry Now (1952)
35) The Filly Wore A Rod (1952)
36) Kill Her If You Can (1952)

SERIES FOUR
37) Murder (1952)
38) Conflict (1952)
39) Tension (1952)
40) Whiplash (1952)
41) Accused (1952)
42) Killer (1952)
43) Suspense (1952)
44) Pursuit (1953)
45) Vengeance (1953)
46) Torment (1953)
47) Amok (1953)
48) Corruption (1953)

SERIES FIVE
49) Silken Menace (1953)
50) Nyloned Avenger (1953)

SPECIALS
Auctioned (1952)
Persian Pride (1952)
Desert Fury (1953)
One Man In His Time (1953)
Unseen Assassin (1953)
Deadly Mission (1953)

KILLER

HANK JANSON

This edition first published in 2004 by
Telos Publishing Ltd
5A Church Road, Shortlands, Bromley, Kent, BR2 0HP,
United Kingdom

www.telos.co.uk

Telos Publishing Ltd values feedback. Please e-mail us with any
comments you may have about this book to: feedback@telos.co.uk

ISBN: 978-1-84583-963-5

Novel by Stephen D Frances
Cover by Reginald Heade
With thanks to Steve Holland
www.hankjanson.co.uk
Cover design by David J Howe

First published in England by New Fiction Press, November 1952

British Library Cataloguing in Publication Data.
A catalogue record for this book is available from the British Library.

PUBLISHER'S NOTE

The appeal of the Hank Janson books to a modern readership lies not only in the quality of the storytelling, which is as powerfully compelling today as it was when they were first published, but also in the fascinating insight they afford into the attitudes, customs and morals of the 1940s and 1950s. We have therefore endeavoured to make *Accused*, and all our other Hank Janson reissues, as faithful to the original editions as possible. Unlike some other publishers, who when reissuing vintage fiction have been known edit it to remove aspects that might offend present-day sensibilities, we have left the original narrative absolutely intact.

The original editions of these classic Hank Janson titles made quite frequent use of phonetic 'Americanisms' such as 'kinda', 'gotta', 'wanna' and so on. Again, we have left these unchanged in the Telos Publishing Ltd reissues, to give readers as genuine as possible a taste of what it was like to read these books when they first came out, even though such devices have since become sorta out of fashion.

The only way in which we have amended the original text has been to correct obvious lapses in spelling, grammar and punctuation – we have, for instance, added question marks in the not-infrequent cases where they were omitted from the ends of questions in the original – and to remedy clear typesetting errors.

Lastly, we should mention that we have made every effort to

trace and acquire relevant copyrights in the various elements that make up this book. However, if anyone has any further information that they could provide in this regard, we would be very grateful to receive it.

INTRODUCTION

Killer was the forty-second Hank Janson novel, originally published in November 1952 and not reprinted until now. Why it became one of the infamous seven Hank Janson books to be prosecuted for obscenity is something of a mystery. Apart from some heavy petting, there's very little in it that could be remotely interpreted as 'depraving' or 'corrupting'. I can only surmise that it was one of the novels the Recorder of London, Gerald Dodson, was referring to when, in his summing up in the trail, he said:

> It was argued [by the defence] that cruelty and brutality alone do not tend to deprave and corrupt. Well, if it were necessary to deal with that, you might, perhaps, think that it might well be that they do both. But we are not concerned with books where cruelty alone and brutality alone figure, because here it is a mixture of sex and cruelty and brutality, and possibly sadism all at the same time.

Killer certainly has elements of sexual tension throughout and, in a separate, unrelated sub-plot, a killer is at large and a girl is murdered when he tries to rub out Hank Janson in a restaurant. Towards the end of the book, Hank beats up an intruder ('I didn't have any pity left in me. I swiped him again, felt the flood of savage satisfaction wash over me when his lips split and blood spurted against my knuckles.'), by far the most graphically brutal scene in the novel.

Although dished out in small doses, the combination – sexual tension, murder and violence – was enough for the book to be condemned as obscene.

For his regular readers, the latest Hank Janson delivered a tried and trusted (if formulaic) story. Hank is racing back towards Chicago when he spies a girl in the headlights and slams on the brakes. Thus we are introduced to Cora, a dim blur in the darkness outside the circle of the car's blazing headlights. As she climbs into the passenger seat, Hank gets tantalising glimpses of her from the dashboard light: 'a glimpse of silk-clad legs and a flash of underclothing as she settled into her seat', 'a pert, cheeky face that was pretty but overpainted.' As the chapter progresses, author Stephen Frances sketches in more details of Cora's physique and personality. Hank reaches for the handbrake ('she swayed her silk-clad knees away from me'), lets out the clutch and starts the car rolling ('She looked at me directly, then, a cool, indifferent, sideways glance. It was the first time I'd seen her eyes … Those eyes revealed two individualities, one pert, pretty, and overpainted; the other fascinating, appealing and intensely provocative'). He invites her to have a cigarette and asks her to light a second one for him ('My lips were greasy with lipstick, the end of the cigarette wet. It was strangely intimate and strangely stirring'), continues driving and glancing over at his passenger. She explains how she ended up stranded at the roadside ('She moved, softly, silkily, crossed one leg over the other, ran her fingers down her silk-sheathed calf'), shows him her broken heel, before reaching down to put her shoe back on ('It was a tight skirt she was wearing, and had ridden up high over her knees. Her underslip was dainty, lace-edged, clean, crisp and tantalisingly intimate').

The conversation counterpoints these tantalising, intimate glimpses of Cora's sexuality. She makes it clear she is not interested in Hank. Cool and indifferent, she explains precisely what she is after in a man:

'I know exactly where I want to get. I know exactly
what I want. Ever since I was a little girl, I've known

exactly what I want.'

'Money?' I guessed, 'plenty of it?'

'Of course.'

'Stashing it away in your stocking every week?'

'You don't get money that way, not the kinda money I want.'

'You know a better way?'

She chuckled. 'The only way a dame can ever get money. By making a man find it for her. I'm waiting until I meet that guy. Then I'm going after him with everything I've got. I'll sink my hooks so deep, he'll never get away.' The strange intensity in her voice was almost frightening.

Despite himself, Hank cannot help but be attracted to her. She is unobtainable, contemptuous and mocking, which far outweighs the fact that Hank sees her, physically, as a 'pretty but not particularly interesting shop girl.' Within a few miles' drive, Cora has set in stone the boundaries of their relationship and bruised Hank's ego … How could he resist such a challenge?

From here on, Hank's sole mission is to cross those boundaries, to prove that her gold-digger attitude is wrong, that 'some day you're gonna marry a guy who earns thirty-five bucks a week, live in a small flat, have dozens of kids and be as happy as you can hope to be.'

Not for the first time, Hank allows emotion to overrule common sense, although not with any romantic 'the heart has its reasons' notions. He does not love Cora. His mixed emotions are a perfect example of cognitive dissonance as first explored by Leon Festinger in 1957. A cognition is an element of knowledge. A second cognition can be related or unrelated. If it is related it can be either consonant or dissonant, strengthening or weakening the first piece of knowledge. Festinger argued that we suppress cognitive dissonance and avoid information likely to increase it; in fact, we will create arguments to support our position. As a heavy smoker, I will argue that I enjoy smoking, that I find it relaxing, that it stops me from gaining more weight; this helps reduce the tension I feel about the fact that smoking will kill me in the long run.

In a similar way, Janson argues his way through his non-existent relationship with Cora. He knows he should not think about her so, of course, he cannot *stop* thinking about her. 'She'd played with me,' recalls Janson, 'taunted me, strung along with me and, finally, with dexterity and skill of a specialist, she'd switched me over from hot to cold, contemptuous and mocking at my weakness.'

He knows that, at any future meeting, the same is likely to happen. But, Janson argues, she is honest and forthright: 'She hadn't tried to spin me a line. She'd put her cards on the table.' He puts her out of his mind, but she keeps coming back. 'I knew I was already half beat, knew that I was gonna have a tough time restraining myself from chasing after her.' When she phones, he cannot resist her offer of a dinner date. He makes excuses to himself for seeing her, and persuades himself that he still has a chance. Anything but admit fully that he is addicted to her because she has dismissed him.

Adding to his problems is Hank's long-standing relationship with fellow *Chicago Chronicle* reporter, Sheila Lang. The red-haired, hot-tempered editoress of the woman's page has been stood-up by Hank before and is not going to stand for it any longer.

To say more would be to give the whole plot away, and I'll end this line of thought by saying that Janson spends the majority of the book in a chaos of mixed emotions, a state few authors would risk, as it comes at the cost of the overall plot.

The themes in *Killer* had all been tackled before by Frances in earlier Janson novels: Janson was hopelessly and irrationally in the thrall of a young heiress, Mindy Hiller, in *This Dame Dies Soon*; and in *Sister, Don't Hate Me*, the beguiling Ruth Lennard is as calculating and materialistic as Cora and just as capable of switching her emotions on and off:

> Her body became dull and lifeless like a rag doll, and
> when my lips sought hers, I found them dry and firm.

I'd reached out to embrace a warm, loveable and exciting woman and found myself clasping a lifeless doll. I let go of her and she asked simply: 'Finished?' (*Sister, Don't Hate Me*, p.75)

Even the frustrated anger of Sheila Lang is nothing new to the Janson saga.

Despite these flaws, *Killer* is still a page-turner. It's one of the few books in the Frances/Janson canon that we have accurate sales figures for: 98,250 copies were sold in just over a year. The sales figures for the novels that immediately followed were also in the 90,000 to 100,000 range, which proves that Frances was delivering the kind of novels his readers wanted, time after time. They loved seeing Hank put through hell, and that's exactly what happens in *Killer*; but this is Frances writing, and his strength was always in his descriptions of interpersonal relationships, of how people attract and repel each other. And sometimes, as Hank is about to find out, it's both at the same time.

Steve Holland
Colchester, March 2004

KILLER

1

She would have passed unnoticed in a crowd, but standing squarely in the road ahead of me the way she was, spotlighted by my headlights like a candidate for the Presidency at a torchlight meeting, there was no avoiding her.

I was travelling at speed. The kinda speed that at night gets you in its grip, the coolness of the night air on your face, the soft, hypnotic purr of the engine humming with subdued vitality, the swish of the tyres a compelling urge to even greater speed, and your headlights cutting into the darkness ahead, carving a clean, white swathe from the surrounding blackness.

I didn't want to stop. I wanted to rocket past her. But the determined way she was standing dead in the centre of the road, legs astride, hands out-thrust as though to stop me, admitted no alternative.

I applied the brakes as I roared towards her, pressed down ever harder as she seemed to be thrown at me, heard my tyres screaming on the tarmac, and smelt the tang of burning brake linings in my nostrils.

I made it, dragged to a reluctant standstill within inches of her. And I was as indignant as any guy has a right to be when compelled to brake savagely to a standstill because of someone's stupidity.

I switched off the engine, wrenched open the car door, stormed around front to where she was waiting for me expectantly.

'You got a suicide clause in your life security?' I demanded harshly.

'I had to be sure you saw me, didn't I?' she snapped, an indignant note in her voice.

I couldn't see her clearly. Only the dim blur of her figure in the darkness beyond the blaze of my headlights.

'Where ya heading? I demanded gruffly, brushing against her in the darkness as I fumbled for the car door, opened it up for her.

I knew from her voice she was tired and irritable. 'Making for Chicago?' she said as she climbed inside, and in the light from the dashboard I caught a glimpse of silk-clad legs and a flash of underclothing as she settled in her seat.

'Going all the way,' I told her.

'Looks like I'm in luck.'

'You sure are,' I gritted. 'Another yard would have made all the difference. They'd have had to shovel you up.'

I went around my side of the car, climbed in behind the steering wheel. I could see her clearly now, in the light radiated from the dashboard. She had a pert, cheeky face that was pretty but over painted. Her thickly-tinted lips made her mouth oversized, and her naturally long eyelashes were spiky, glued together with mascara.

I switched on the engine, reached down and released the hand-brake situated between us. Quickly, just a little too quickly, she swayed her silk-clad knees away from me.

'You scared or somethin'?' I grated irritably. She tugged at the hem of her skirt, tried to pull it down over her knees. She didn't succeed, because it wasn't long enough. I noticed her knees were neatly rounded and dimpled.

'Maybe we oughta get it straightened out right away,' she said tonelessly.

'Get what straightened out?'

'A fella took me out tonight,' she said emotionlessly. 'To dance ... he said! But he got fresh and ...' She shrugged her shoulder.

'And ...' I prompted.

'Use your imagination,' she snapped irritably. 'I preferred to walk.'

I figured the guy musta been mighty ambitious. She looked to me the sort of dame who would have to be good and worried before she started walking. Moreover, she didn't look the type who worried easy.

I let in the clutch, started rolling. As I built up speed, I said from the corner of my mouth: 'You don't have to worry about me. I'm the kinda guy who likes cooperation.'

'Let's hope you stay that way long enough to get me back to Chicago.'

The note of bored confidence in her voice got me rattled. 'Who do you figure you are, anyway?' I grated. 'Venus?'

She looked at me directly, then, a cool, indifferent, sideways glance. It was the first time I'd seen her eyes, and all at once I knew everything could be the way she was hinting. It wasn't that her eyes were beautiful. Sure, they were large and clear. But there was something more. Much more. Almost as though her eyes were a forbidden promise, hinting at a real *her* hidden behind a layer of paint and powder. Those eyes revealed two individualities, one pert, pretty and overpainted; the other, fascinating, appealing and intensely provocative.

It was a glance that lasted but a moment, then she was staring through the windscreen at the searchlighted road ahead. But things weren't the same any more. She had changed subtly and provocatively in a split second.

My hands were sweaty on the steering wheel and my mouth dry. Suddenly I realised I'd been holding my breath for a long time. I exhaled slowly, fumbled in my pocket for a cigarette, and as my elbow brushed her arm, she flinched away from me.

'Cigarette?' I invited.

'If you like.' Her voice was cool and indifferent. She made no secret her only interest in me was cheap transport to town. There wasn't the slightest hint of friendliness in her voice.

I passed her the pack. She took a cigarette, passed the pack back.

'Light one for me,' I asked. 'There's sharp bends on this road.'

She shot me a sideways glance, took the pack from me again, placed two cigarettes between her lips.

'There's a lighter fitted to the dashboard,' I told her.

She used it.

I tried to watch her and the road at the same time. I began to feel maybe I'd been imagining things. Her profile confirmed my first impression, a pert, cheeky, overpainted shop assistant type. I began to breathe more freely, knew I must have been imagining things.

Then she leaned towards me, placed the cigarette between my lips. I had the smell of her in my nostrils then, the cheap perfume from a ten-cent store, cheap face powder and hair shampoo. And something more. A subtle fragrance of something that was intimately her.

My lips were greasy with lipstick, the end of the cigarette wet. It was strangely intimate and strangely stirring. I said, gruffly: 'What you do? Chew cigarettes?'

'What d'you want I should do? Smoke it for you as well?'

I glanced at her in the same moment she glanced at me. I hadn't been mistaken that first time after all. It was all there in her eyes, allure, promise and other things. Almost everything that a guy could want.

She turned her eyes away from me quickly, and it was like a conjuring trick, transforming her again into that cheeky, pertly pretty and not particularly interesting shop girl.

I swallowed hard, said gruffly: 'Had you been waiting long?'

'I don't know,' she said, disinterestedly. 'Maybe an hour. Three cars passed. None of them stopped.'

'So when I came along, you made sure of me?'

'I had to do something. I didn't want to spend all night on the road.' She moved, softly, silkily, crossed one leg over the other, ran her fingers down her silk-sheathed calf, fumbled, came up with a dainty, black suede shoe that was good for ballroom dancing but hopeless for a stroll around the block.

'Look at that!' she said disgustedly. I looked. The heel was maybe six inches high, except the shoe hadn't got a heel!

'How far d'you figure I'd get with that?' she asked.

'Have you got the heel?'

'Nope.'

'How come you lost it?'

She gave a sigh of exasperation. 'Didn't I tell you? This guy got fresh, see. We played ring-a-ring of roses around his car until I took off into the bushes. I tripped on a root, lost my heel, and right then it wasn't convenient to stop and find it. Savvy? Right then he was so hot for me he'd have burned me up too, if he'd got so much as one hand on me.'

'Where d'ya live, kid?'

She didn't answer right away. She was thrusting her dainty foot back into that heelless shoe. It was a tight skirt she was wearing, and had ridden up high over her knees. Her underslip was dainty, lace-edged, clean, crisp and tantalisingly intimate.

'Where d'you live, kid?' I asked again, as she straightened up.

'If you're gonna drop me home, that's gonna be right fine,' she told me.

'Sure,' I said. 'I'll drop you home. It's late for a dame to be wandering around alone.'

Again her eyes flashed at me, eyes that this time contained a hint of mockery as though she was secretly amused I should be concerned for her safety.

'We'll be hitting the outskirts of town in twenty minutes,' I said, and was inwardly angry she should have such an effect upon me. She was just a dame, just an ordinary, commonplace dame, the sort of dame you can meet any time on Michigan Avenue. Nothing special about her except … those eyes!

'What's your line,' she asked.

'I'm a writer … of sorts!'

She sniffed contemptuously. 'You can't make a fortune that way!'

'I don't aim to. I wouldn't know what to do with a fortune if I had it.'

Again a momentary flash from those expressive eyes, mockery and amusement blended in a calculated cynicism that was startling in its wiseness.

'You've got to alter your idea if you want to get somewhere,' she told me, like she was a department head giving advice to the office boy.

'Maybe you and me don't wanna get the same place.'

She said, in a determined voice: 'I know exactly where I want to get. I know exactly what I want. Ever since I was a little girl, I've known exactly what I want.'

'Money?' I guessed. 'Plenty of it?'

'Of course.'

'Stashing it away in your stocking week by week?'

'You don't get money that way, not the kinda money I want.'

'You know a better way?'

She chuckled. 'The only way a dame can ever get money. By making a man find it for her. I'm waiting until I meet that guy. Then I'm going after him, I'll go after him with everything I've got. I'll sink my hooks so deep, he'll never get away.' The strange intensity in her voice was almost frightening.

I took a deep breath. 'At least you're honest. I guess other dames feel that way, but wild horses would never make them admit it.'

'I don't see any reason to hide it. Just show me a guy who can flash a bankroll big enough, and I'll go gunning for him.'

I slammed into a sharp curve, had to brake and swing hard on the steering wheel as the tyres screeched a protest.

She rocked towards me, her shoulder thrusting against my forearm, her thigh and knee pressing hard against mine. I straightened up, and momentarily she stayed the way she was, her body pressing against mine so I tingled all over, felt my hands slippery on the steering wheel and my lips surprisingly hot and dry.

She pushed away from me.

It was like my skin was being peeled away from me.

'You're a nice kid,' I said hoarsely. 'Why do you have to talk so tough? You know you don't mean what you've been saying.'

Her chuckle was scornful and contemptuous. 'Just show me a guy with dough,' she said. You'll see if I mean it.'

I took another sharp curve at speed, but this time she braced herself, barely touched me.

'Some day you're gonna marry a guy who earns thirty-five bucks a week, live in a small flat, have dozens of kids and be as happy as you can hope to be.'

'You kidding?' she said scornfully.

'Just philosophising. That's the way life works out.'

There was irony and mockery in her voice now. 'You ain't aiming to be that guy?'

I ignored the question, swung into another steep turn, crested a hill and saw the distant lights of Chicago gleaming far ahead of me. Then I was cruising down hill, headlights picking out the road ahead of me, outlining the bridge below and casting a brilliant sheen across the silent waters of the river.

At first I thought it was a shadow. But she had seen it, too. Was leaning forward in her seat, lips half-parted.

I rammed my foot down hard on the gas. 'Did you see what I saw?' I rasped.

'Yeah. She jumped just before the headlights hit her.'

We were swooping down towards the bridge now at a dangerous speed. But I didn't slacken off. There are times when even seconds may prove to be a fatal delay. I hurled the car at the bridge, hit a bump which made me slew half way across the road, wrenched on the steering wheel, straightened up and stood on the brakes with everything I had.

They were good brakes, and I'd had practice in using them. It was the second time that night I'd had to use them hard. I was tensed, ready for the skidding halt. But she wasn't. Her head hit the windscreen – and hard!

A bang on the forehead was nothing to worry about at such a time. I was out of the car almost before it had stopped. A hat and handbag were splayed on the sidewalk at the edge of the parapet, and they were all the proof I needed.

I placed my hands on the bridge parapet, vaulted, saw the glint of the dark waters far below me as I mentally charged myself with being a dope, for jumping crazily, without looking first to make sure no boat was underneath on which I could pulp myself.

2

My imagination played tricks with me, because it wasn't all that high. It seemed I was falling never-endingly before the soles of my shoes slapped the surface of the water.

Ice-cold wetness enveloped me with a whoosh. I was going down and down into never-ending blackness, the biting cold sucking flesh from my body, driving hard against my eardrums, the wet embrace, clamping me ever tighter and tighter. Then, when I had almost abandoned hope and believed I would plunge ever deeper and deeper until my body embedded itself in the mud of the bed of the river, I realised I was no longer sinking, was surfacing like a submarine, ever and ever more rapidly.

My head broke water and I bobbed up, clear almost to my hips.

I shook my head to clear my eyes of water, blinked, peered through the surrounding darkness. My clothes clung around me like leaden shrouds, dragging me down like a diver's boots.

Then I saw her, just a few yards away from me, struggling desperately.

She wasn't struggling for the reason you'd have thought. She wasn't struggling for life, making the frantic movements of a drowning person.

She was struggling to drown!

She'd been wearing a pleated skirt when she jumped and it had opened up like a parachute, ballooned, so that when she hit the water the air within it was imprisoned, formed an inflated lifebelt which was preventing her from sinking.

And she was struggling to release the air from her skirt so she would sink!

She succeeded just before I reached her. Air bubbled out from beneath the skirt and she sank at once.

The will to live is deeply implanted in everyone. Until that moment she'd probably been quite determined on committing suicide – mentally.

But when the cold water closed in on her and the cold hand of death clutched at her throat with a greedy, suffocating strength, reason vanished and the blind, panic-instinct of the will-to-live overcame her mental desires.

I was there waiting when her head bobbed above the surface. I grabbed a handful of hair, held it tight. Her hands were frantic and grasping, clawing the water like it had substance. She tried to scream, and water slopped into her mouth, made her splutter and choke, terrified her so that her frantic splashings were re-doubled.

I tried to swim around back of her and get a grip on her shoulders. Her arms were thrashing wildly, and one blindly searching hand found me, found a straw that could be clutched. Her nails gouged into my flesh and her terrified, drowning strength was enveloping me with a determination that only a drowning person possesses. Her legs and arms clamped around me grimly, gripped like iron bands in an embrace that would never relax, that would endure while breath lasted.

It wasn't a pleasant experience. I myself was touched by the shadow of panic. My clothes, soaked and heavy with water, were a leaden weight steadily sapping my strength. Her iron grip was the grip of a watery death.

And with her arms and legs twined around me, my desperate efforts to keep afloat were fast sapping my remaining strength.

You can read in books how easy it is to save a drowning person. You can read how, in an emergency, the rescuer can neatly uppercut the panic-stricken drowning person, tow them unconscious to the shore with confident ease.

But that's in books!

Imagine for yourself, arms heavy and weighed down by soaked clothing, and no firm ground to pivot upon as you swing your fist. Any guy who can swing a knock-out punch under such circumstances is either a superman a liar.

I'd handled this all wrong. I shoulda approached slowly from behind, grabbed her ears and towed her gently but firmly to the shore.

But it hadn't worked out that way. She was clinging to me like a limpet and I wasn't ever gonna shake her loose.

I still had a little strength left, and my mind was still working. There's only one reason why a drowning person clutches a straw. Because the straw is floating. I exhaled air from my lungs, became limp and deliberately allowed myself to sink.

She went down with me. I heard her choked splutter a moment before we went under. And then I was sinking, sinking, sinking, and all the time the dragging grip and the weight of her body was the greedy embrace of a giant octopus. It needed great mental effort not to struggle with her, to remain limp, and allow myself to sink deeper and deeper, until, at the last moment, when fearing my lungs would burst, the instinct for survival exerted itself inside her and she released me, clawed madly at the water, trying to climb up through it to the life-giving air above.

I kicked away from her, surfaced maybe a coupla yards away. This time, I approached her warily.

She musta been half-drowned anyway. She choked, wheezed as her waterlogged lungs tried to suck in air, and her arms seemed to have lost their strength, because she went down again.

This time, I was watching carefully, and was right behind her when she surfaced. I grabbed her firmly by the head, my hands pressed hard over her ears, and hooked my little fingers below her jaw, holding her head like it was in a vice. Her hands came up automatically, clawed desperately, and her body squirmed as she tried to turn around to get another firm grip on me.

But I was kicking out now, swimming on my back, kicking hard and towing her along with me. I maintained a tight grip on her head and kept kicking.

It was like I was dragging lead. The water was lapping around me greedily, the weight of my clothes sucking me down and down, and my breath was rasping in my throat. I shot a quick glance over my shoulder, and through the darkness could vaguely see the dim outline of the shore.

It seemed a hundred miles away.

I shut my eyes, gritted my teeth and kept on kicking.

She was a half-submerged log, heavy with water, struggling just a little, still partly conscious and still a threat to our lives. I wasn't even sure now that I could make it.

I closed my eyes, summoned my remaining strength and kept kicking with leaden legs.

It was an eternity of dull, leaden misery, with the growing conviction that I wasn't going to make it.

My head was sinking lower and lower, water washing over my face, swirling into my nose and mouth, making me cough and splutter, choking me so that every breath was a pained effort.

I'd been in the water for hours now, resolutely kicking out with leaden legs that were sinking. I was crazy to have attempted to save her. I wasn't gonna make it. I had maybe one or two more kicks left in me, and then my strength would give out.

Then she was there, a hand grasping my shoulder, tugging at me, her voice telling me everything was okay. My leaden legs sank, touched bottom, and I felt faint with relief. I wanted to haul myself up the river bank, sprawl there like a seal in the sun, cough the water up from out of my lungs and draw in deep breaths of life-giving air.

But I hadn't time to spare. I had a half-drowned woman on my hands. Between us, we dragged her up the bank. She was barely conscious. I rolled her over on her belly, put her head on one side, sat astride her and rammed the heels of my palms hard into the small of her back with a rhythmical breathing movement.

She sure had swallowed a lotta water. And she was going through hell, coughing and choking, blue in the face, water and vomit filtering out from between her twisted lips. I kept hard at it, bearing down on her, crushing unmercifully with the weight of my body and the urgency of my hands. But it was justified. She wasn't going to die.

Not this time, anyway!

'There's a blanket in the back of my car,' I instructed crisply. 'Get it for me. You'll find a torch in the dash-box and a bottle of brandy. Bring those too.'

She didn't waste time with questions. She disappeared into the gloom, leaving me to continue my efforts. And I was sweating now, despite the coldness of the water, could feel my clothes drying on me, almost steaming.

When she got back, the other dame was breathing stentorously, whimpering a little and moaning a little. I spread the blanket, rolled her over on to it, wrapped it around her and forced brandy between her clenched lips. It had an almost immediate effect. I wasn't mean with the brandy. I poured almost a quarter of a bottle into her. It brought colour to her cheeks, eased her breathing, enabled her to go limp and relaxed.

I got up slowly, feeling stiff and weak, and gave her the once-over in the light of my flashlamp. With her soaked hair splayed over her forehead and her make-up washed off, it was hard to tell her age. I figured she was maybe thirty-five.

'Can you figure why she should want to throw herself in the river?' she asked over my shoulder, in her indifferent voice.

I glanced around at her, remembered that she was still with me. 'Lots of folks have troubles,' I said.

'Not this dame,' she said crisply. 'Look at those rings she's wearing, and look at her clothes. She must be lousy with dough.'

'It's like I told you,' I said. 'Dough ain't everything.'

'What do you reckon to get out of this, anyway? A medal?'

'Quit being so mercenary,' I sighed wearily. 'Find a phone

box and bring the cops.'

She turned the flashlight on my face, held it so it half-blinded me. I could sense her watching me calculatingly. 'Maybe that ain't such a good idea. You know what happens to attempted suicides? They get put on the stand, maybe sent down for a nine months' rap.'

'What other ideas have you got?'

She angled the flashlamp, held it so she could open up a handbag, rifle through its contents. 'This bag is hers,' she explained. 'Musta dropped it before she jumped.'

I caught a glimpse of a roll of crisp greenbacks, and a gold cigarette case. 'Cut that out,' I snarled swiftly. 'I'm not gonna stand for you rolling the dame while she's unconscious.'

'Hold it, hold it,' she sneered. 'I've told you already that I'm after the big money. I'm not interested in peanuts. And any dough I get, I want on the square; and plenty of it.' She found what she was looking for: a visiting card. 'This will tell us who she is,' she said with satisfaction. She held the card between two gracefully arched fingers, read aloud: *'Mrs Rosa and Frank Greigs, Treetops, Chicago.'*

'You suggesting we should take her back home?' I asked. 'It can't be far from here, she walked.'

'It would be doing her a favour, at that.'

I shrugged. 'You'll have to give me a hand with her.'

The dame was still moaning, shivering now like she had the ague. I worked my hands under her shoulders, lifted. ''Take her feet,' I instructed. Between us, we stumbled I up the steep banks, carried her to my car, wrestled her inside and propped her up on the back seat.

I was breathing heavily by the time we were through.

She said: 'I should take a shot of that brandy yourself, if you don't wanna catch a cold.'

I took a shot. A good strong shot. Enough to make me shudder.

'After you,' she said.

That was when I noticed she was soaked to the waist, shivering from the cold of the early morning air.

'Better get her home quick,' I rasped. 'All three of us can do with a brisk towelling.'

It took twenty minutes to find the Greigs' joint. It was tucked away in a side road that led to nowhere, the kinda joint a guy chooses who wants dignified and expensive seclusion. A high brick wall surrounded the grounds, and a long, sweeping drive led up to a Georgian mansion that was big enough to house a dozen families.

There were so many lights burning I'd have thought there was a Grand Ball in progress, if it hadn't been that as soon as the sound of my car was heard, the door burst open and three agitated and worried men came running out to meet me. Almost as soon as I'd applied the brakes and brought the car to a standstill at the foot of the steps, they were crowding around me.

'Have you got her?' demanded a worried voice. 'Did you find her?'

The light streaming down from the front door glinted on his silvery hair, showed his worried blue eyes and the anxiety written on his lined face.

'You Mr Greigs?' I countered.

That was when he realised I was a stranger. 'Yeah,' he said. 'That's right. Forgive me, I mistook you for someone else.' He fluttered his hands nervously. 'You see I'm very worried about my wife and ...'

I jerked my thumb over my shoulder towards the back of the car. 'Don't worry any longer. She's here. And what she needs right now is a warm bed and a doctor.'

'Thank God,' he breathed.

And then it hit me. He was white-haired, maybe sixty-five. Old enough to be her father.

And she was his *wife*!

3

Greigs acted like his wife was the most important factor in his life. His worry and concern for her was almost heartbreaking. The other two men, who by their conversation proved themselves relatives, gently lifted her out of the car, while Greigs himself fussed around like an old hen, without the strength to help, but fluttery and anxious.

They carried her inside the house and up the stairs. We trailed along behind, and one guy suddenly remembered us. 'Would you mind waiting in there?' he asked, nodding towards a door leading off the entrance hall. 'We'd like to have a talk with you.'

'Sure,' I agreed. 'We'll wait.'

We entered the room, and a few moments later the door was closed behind us. I looked at the girl, raised my eyebrows expressively, shrugged my shoulders.

She growled, 'Hell, I'm cold.'

She was, too; her lips blue, her teeth chattering.

I glanced around the room. It was expensively furnished, and with good taste. A grand piano stood at the far end of the room on a raised dais, bearing a large framed photograph of Mrs Greigs.

I crossed over to it, stood studying the photograph. The photographer had made an excellent job of it, made her look maybe twenty-five. And beautiful!

She slipped off her shoes, came up behind me quietly. I

didn't know she was there until I heard the chattering of her teeth. 'Makes her a real movie queen,' she said contemptuously.

I turned and stared at her, and got the full impact of her eyes, looking directly into mine.

It was incredible how eyes alone could transform her from a very ordinary girl into someone of special significance for me!

I started sweating, wondered what was coming over me. A slow, triumphant smile flickered around her lips, which she made no attempt to conceal. And I knew right away she hadn't been talking foolishly. Any time she wanted to go for a guy in a big way, she could get him hog-tied with those eyes.

'What's your name?' I said, thickly.

'Cora. Why d'ya wanna know?'

'What else?'

'The name's Cora. That's a long enough handle for you. D'you want I should write you my biography?'

I was still sweating, my damp clothes clinging to me, chilling my sweat, making me uncomfortable. I wrenched my eyes away from hers, looked around the room. There was a cocktail cabinet on the far side. 'I figure we could both do with a slug of brandy,' I muttered.

She followed me over to the cabinet, stood watching me while I poured. From the corner of my eye, I studied her.

Everything about her was shop girl. The cheap material of her costume skirt and jacket, her stockings, and the make-up painted thickly on her pert, cheeky face. Even her perfume was cheap.

She sipped the brandy gratefully, but her teeth still chattered. Her fingers were white and numb, her wet skirt clung to her and outlined the curves of her parted thighs. Her jacket sleeves were damp.

I peeled off my jacket, spread it over the back of a chair. 'I hope these guys aren't gonna be too long,' I muttered. 'I need a change and a brisk towelling.'

'I'm numbed right through to the bone,' she chattered.

'Be smart then,' I said. 'Slip off that coat and let it dry.'

Her eyes still wore that same, strange, mocking expression. 'I think I'll keep it on,' she said.

'You're wet through.'

She took another sip at her brandy. 'Listen, fella,' she rasped. 'When you picked me up, I was walking. Remember?'

'Sure,' I agreed, puzzled.

'So that's why.'

I still didn't get it. 'What's that got to do with taking off your coat?'

She was young, maybe twenty or twenty-two. But her eyes were worldly and knowledgeable, wise far beyond her years. 'Do I have to draw a picture?' she sneered.

'Yeah,' I rasped. 'I'm dumb.'

There was still that mocking smile curling her lips as she finished drinking her brandy, carefully replaced the glass on the cocktail tray, and with swift, nimble fingers, unbuttoned her jacket, opened it wide, half jerked it off over her shoulders.

She'd been wearing a Hungarian type blouse. But she wasn't any longer, because most of the front of it had been ripped away, torn clean out, leaving only ragged edges. Maybe she'd been wearing a brassiere too. But if she had, there was no sign of it now.

And those eyes!

Those eyes, mocking and all knowing!

I stared, gulped, became icy-cold, and then started to sweat. Because all the time her eyes were watching me mockingly, laughing, contemptuous and all-wise, subtly enjoying my reactions.

'He did … that?' I gulped.

'You get the idea now, huh?'

'Yeah,' I said, hoarsely. The sweat was gathering in my eyebrows.

'What's eating you?' she sneered. 'You've been around, ain't you?'

'Yeah,' I said, weakly.

'A dame's body ain't no novelty to a guy like you.'

'No,' I gulped.

'What's biting you then?'

What answer can a guy give to a question like that?

Especially when a dame asks the question.

Could you say that the taut, pointed freshness of firm flesh was breathtaking, that the rounded ripeness was exerting an almost overwhelming fascination, that youthful vitality and crispness and feminine magnetism were making your hands tremble, heating your blood and stimulating desire to see more and yet more?

'I guess I'm running a fever,' I croaked.

She didn't believe it any more than I did. Her eyes were mocking and laughing yet pleased as she pulled her jacket back over her shoulders and started buttoning. She buttoned the lowest button first, not once moving her eyes from me while she did it. It was a kinda sweet torment as she buttoned slowly, deliberately tantalising me, tugging at my sensory emotions until I was trembling all over.

'What a pushover you'd be for a dame who wants to get her claws into you,' she rasped critically.

I kinda shuddered. She'd fastened the last button now. But her eyes were still fastened on me, kinda drawing the strength outta me. 'If you got that fella feeling the way I feel now, it's not surprising he chased you around.'

She chuckled. A cool, calculated chuckle. 'I know it all, fella,' she said confidently. 'I know it all. I can work on a guy like he's a musical instrument, make him jive any tune I want, get him sweating away on the top note and make him hold it. I can switch it off, too. Just like that.' She snapped her fingers. 'I can make a guy feel cooler than an iceberg and as dead as a mortuary client in five seconds-flat.'

I could breathe more easily now. 'Like the guy who's got the front of your blouse,' I gritted.

She chuckled ruefully. 'One of my few mistakes. I overshot myself.'

'Hardly a fatal miscalculation, after so much practice,' I said bitterly.

Her eyes flashed angrily. Deep down in them I could see tiny sparks of anger glowing redly. 'Just how wrong can guys like you be?' she snarled. 'D'you think I'm dope enough to make myself cheap? D'you think I'm gonna waste myself?' She was angrily indignant. 'I'm not giving myself away, fella. Not until I meet the guy who's got what I want. He can have me if he wants. But only when I've got what I'm after.'

'In the meantime it's just … practice!' I taunted.

She flushed slightly. 'What do you take me for? A call girl!'

'Maybe you're not so far off, at that,' I said, bitterly. 'The difference is that you're aiming for the top. You sell yourself just once. For the biggest price you can get.'

She nearly smacked my face. Her eyes were furious, and only a determined effort to control herself saved me.

'Why you getting so sore?' I taunted. 'I'm only expressing in different words what you told me yourself.'

She was breathing hard, fighting me with her eyes. Then, quite suddenly, she looked away from me, shrugged her shoulders. 'Okay, fella,' she said, with a careless air. 'If that's the way you see it, there's nothing I can do about it.'

'Nothing except keep your claws good and long, well sharpened and ready for use.'

She ignored that crack, glanced around the room critically. 'Seems like this Greigs fella must be in the real dough.'

'Sure,' I agreed. 'But he's already got a wife. He doesn't look to me the kinda guy who would commit bigamy.'

'He's kinda strong for that dame, isn't he?' she asked.

'It happens with married folk. Sometimes!'

'I wonder why she wanted to kill herself,' she added thoughtfully.

It was the question I'd been asking myself all the time. But before I could answer, there came a tap at the door, it opened and a short, podgy, fleshy-faced guy wearing tails and a boiled shirt-front glided into the room. From the emotionless expression on his face and the unbending frigidity of his pose, we knew right away he was a butler of sorts.

He purred, softly and smoothly: 'If you will be so good as to accompany me …'

We followed him out into the vast hall, up the long,

sweeping staircase that was ankle-deep in carpet, and along one of the upper-floor corridors.

He opened one door, bowed from the waist and purred: 'This is for the young lady. Everything she needs should be here. If there is anything she lacks, there is a bell.'

Cora shot me a cynical smile, passed in through the door and closed it behind her.

I followed the butler along the corridor, found myself being shown into another room. A large bedroom with a bathroom annexe.

He said: 'If there is anything you want, you have only to ring.'

He disappeared smoothly, like he was wearing rubber-tyred skates, closing the door so softly I had to check to make sure it was really closed.

Yeah, Cora had been right. This guy Greigs sure had dough. I was betting the bedroom furnishing alone musta cost a small fortune. And the bathroom was like a Sultan's palace, black and white tiles with every luxurious convenience that could be desired.

I climbed out of my clothes, got under the shower and stayed there for almost twenty minutes, washing away the damp and the sweat and the smell of the river. I emerged feeling fit and healthy, towelled myself briskly and stepped back into the bedroom to see what arrangements had been made for me.

There was nothing I lacked. Everything was provided. Silken pyjamas, slippers, and a dressing gown that fitted perfectly. And, as though he had been hovering outside, gauging my movements with uncanny foresight, the butler knocked at the door in that same moment.

'If you will let me have your clothes,' he purred, 'I'll see they are dried and pressed.' He gathered them up carefully, like they were the robes of a king.

'And if it is convenient, sir, Mr Greigs would like to see you,' he added.

'That's okay,' I told him. 'I'm not busy right now.'

'If you will kindly follow me, sir.'

It seemed like I was spending most of my time in this house following this dressed-up turkey around.

It was to the library he conducted me this time, a vast room lined with books, each book bound and gold embossed on the spine with the same motif and Greigs' initials.

She was already waiting there, brooding over the pages of a fashion magazine. She glanced up as I came in, lifted one disdainful eyebrow.

The butler withdrew quietly, closing the door behind him silently.

'Well?' she said.

'Mr Greigs wants to see us,' I purred, smoothly.

She tossed the magazine to one side, climbed to her feet gracefully, stood poising herself. 'Get a load of this negligee,' she invited.

I gave it the once-over. It was too big for, her but I knew what she was getting at. It was beautifully tailored from expensive material. In short – it had cost plenty!

'And these too,' she said, admiringly, opening up the negligee so I could see the black silk pyjamas, beautifully embroidered in gold silks.

'Exactly the kind of good quality clothing you're gonna buy when you get your claws into a guy with dough,' I said bitterly.

She said, artfully: 'Greigs's got dough, hasn't he?'

I strode across to her, stared down into her eyes. 'What does that crack mean?' I demanded, roughly.

She smiled impishly, turned away from me, played with the cord of her negligee. 'We saved his wife's life, didn't we? He oughta feel grateful.'

I grabbed her wrist, crushed it between my fingers. 'You little bitch,' I rasped. 'Forget those kinda ideas. You can't put a price on human life that way.'

'Lemme go,' she snarled. 'You're hurting.' And her face was suddenly contorted with anger, lips writhing, eyes flashing.

'Just don't step outta line,' I rasped, and released her hand like it was a poisonous snake.

She stood there, rubbing her wrist, glaring at me angrily. Yet despite the glowing anger in those eyes, they were getting me again, lapping at me steadily like the silent, remorseless rising of a flood.

'What's it to you anyway?' she snarled.

'Nothing,' I said, hoarsely. 'But lay off the guy, will ya? Can't you see he's worried about his wife?'

Suddenly the anger was gone from her eyes, and a mocking smile was curling her lips. 'Hell,' she said, contemptuously, 'it's just like I said. You're a hundred per cent sucker for a dame.'

The hell of it was, she was right. Moreover, I knew I was becoming a sucker for her. She had something, this dame. Nothing at all to recommend her except her eyes. But those eyes were getting me, making me want her, making me anxious for her, making me figure out all kinds of reasons why she should change her attitude to life, and knowing all the time, deep down inside me, that basically I wanted her for myself.

It was at that moment the door opened and Greigs himself came in. His face was haggard, there were bags beneath his eyes, and his shoulders drooped dejectedly. His lined face and white hair made him appear even older than I had at first thought him to be. Accompanying him were the two fellas who had assisted Mrs Greigs upstairs to bed. One was tall, broad-shouldered and with a tiny wisp of a moustache. He had a sturdy physique, but a feminine softness about his features that indicated a weak character. Greigs introduced him as his wife's brother, Tony Gilmore. The other guy, shorter and thick-set, was a friend of the family. He rent by the name of Warren Anderson.

When the introductions were completed, Greigs wrinkled his brow, looked at me thoughtfully. 'I seem have heard your name before, somewhere. Hank Janson rings a bell.'

'Maybe you read the *Chicago Chronicle*?'

'I read all the newspapers. Have you been in the news recently ...' He broke off, stared at me with eyes suddenly wide and apprehensive. 'Wait a minute. Of course. I understand now. You're Hank Janson of the *Chronicle*.'

'That's right,' I admitted.

I was acutely conscious that Cora was staring at me wide-eyed. And there was something more than interest in her eyes. I felt myself flush.

Tony Gilmore said: 'I've read any amount of your stuff, Mr Janson. It is indeed a real pleasure meeting you and ...'

Greigs interrupted anxiously, and there was desperation in his voice. 'Please, Mr Janson. I really must beg of you.' His anxious hands fluttered nervously. 'I had hoped there would be no publicity, but now ...'

'About your wife?' I said, quietly.

He clenched his fists tightly, and for a moment I was scared he was gonna burst into tears. His shoulders drooped even more. 'I suppose you want to print this. Everything.'

'You've got the wrong idea, Mr Greigs. Sure, I'm a reporter. It's my job to report news. But it's not my job to crucify folk. I don't have to put the finger on people who've already got plenty of trouble.'

He stared at me with new hope shining in his eyes. 'You mean ...' he breathed. 'You mean that you don't have to print anything about this?'

'If it means all that much to you, no.'

He gave a sigh of relief, suddenly remembered he was the host. 'Get Miss Tanter and Mr Janson a drink, Tony,' he instructed. 'What would you like, Mr Janson?'

'Scotch,' I said.

'Bourbon,' said Cora, loudly and promptly.

'I think I owe you an explanation, Mr Janson. You see, when my wife ...'

'How is she?' I interrupted. 'What does the doctor say?'

'She's going to be all right,' he said, with relief. 'She's suffering from shock now and has possibly caught a chill. But she's wrapped up warm, and the doctor's given her a sleeping draught. She should be all right this time tomorrow.'

'Well enough to attempt it all over again?' I said, dryly.

Tony Gilmore got back with the drinks in time to hear my last crack. He shot a quick glance at Greigs and another at

Warren Anderson. Then he dropped his eyes quickly, veiled them as though afraid I could read what was in his mind. Greigs said, worriedly: 'I'm afraid this must all seem very strange to you, Mr Janson.'

'Nothing seems strange to a newspaper man. He gets used to the queerest things.'

'I've had a very worrying time,' he explained, tiredly. 'My wife, who is an orphan, recently lost her uncle and aunt in a car accident, and since then has not been herself. Her health has to be watched over very carefully.'

'You mean she's half-cracked,' I said bluntly.

He flinched at that, then slowly nodded his head in agreement. 'I myself would not have put it quite so strongly, but I must admit that temporarily she is suffering from mental strain.'

I took a deep breath. 'You've got a responsibility to your wife, Mr Greigs. She nearly pulled it off tonight. I don't know how many times she's tried it before, but the chances are she's gonna try again. The next time you might not be so lucky. There may be nobody around to help her.'

He said, worriedly: 'There's so much in what you say. Rosa has tried it before. But the doctors are quite certain that with complete rest, within a few months she'll be her normal self again. Meantime ...' He looked from Tony Gilmore to Warren Anderson. 'I have her brother and our good friend Warren Anderson to help me. For two months now, she's never been out of our sight. Until tonight, that is, when due to a misunderstanding, she left the house without us knowing.'

'And what's happening now?' I demanded. 'Could be she's climbing down the drainpipe or throwing herself from the window.'

'The windows are screwed shut,' he said, quietly. 'They are filled with unbreakable, glass and the door is locked from the outside. We have taken every precaution. There is no way she can do herself an injury while she is within her bedroom.'

'There are such things as sanatoriums,' I pointed out.

He nodded his head slowly. 'I'm obliged to accept the advice of my medical advisors. They feel, and probably quite rightly, that Rosa will find her way back to health more quickly in surroundings she knows and understands. All I want is that she should recover her health as quickly as possible.'

'That's all anyone could want,' I told him. 'And don't worry about me. I shan't print any of this. You've got my word for that.'

'It's very kind of you,' he said, sincerely.

Cora said suddenly, her pert face jutting forward aggressively: 'He was going to call in the cops. It was my idea to bring your wife home.'

Greigs turned to her, stared like he was seeing her for the first time. 'That was very nice of you indeed,' he said, and there was a guarded note in his voice, as though he could read what was at the back of her mind.

'Yeah, it was her idea,' I said. 'I was all for calling the cops. But she looked in your wife's handbag, found a visiting card.'

'For that I am very grateful,' he said, sincerely. 'The publicity would have done me no good, and may have resulted in Rosa being legally compelled to enter a sanatorium. I fear that would have been the last straw for her.'

Warren Anderson said quietly: 'Would you mind telling us how it happened, Mr Janson?'

I told him everything. They listened intently, and when I was through, Greigs took my hand, squeezed it hard. 'You don't know what this means to me,' he said, with a break in his voice. 'If anything had happened to Rosa, I don't know what I should have done.'

Tony Gilmore said: 'I owe you something, too. She's my sister.'

'Skip it,' I said, gruffly. 'I only did what anyone would have done.'

'But you've gone to a lot of trouble to help me,' said Greigs. 'Your clothes have been ruined, and you've put yourself out considerably. Please do let me reimburse you for any loss you have suffered.'

'It's okay,' I said. 'Skip it. It wasn't anything. Maybe

sometime, someday, you'll do the same for me.'

He sighed. 'I would like to show my thanks in some way. If there is anything I can do at any time …'

'Sure,' I said. 'I'll remember.'

'And you too, young lady,' Greigs added.

She looked at him, and I could see her eyes calculating and thoughtful. 'It's all right, Mr Greigs. I did what any dame would have done.'

'And don't forget, young lady. If at any time …'

She interrupted, said reluctantly: 'Well, Mr Greigs, there is one thing …' She broke off.

I glared at her, narrowed one eye menacingly.

'Yes?' encouraged Greigs. 'What is it?'

'It doesn't matter,' she said quickly. 'Forget it. It's not important at all.'

She was acting her part well. Greigs blundered, foolishly followed the bait.

'I insist. You must tell me. What is it you wanted to say?'

"It's nothing. Nothing at all.'

'But I insist, young lady.'

'It's just that …' She broke off again, shrugged her shoulders. 'It's difficult to say it.'

'Young lady,' he said, sincerely. 'My wife is upstairs in bed, alive and as well as can be expected. If it hadn't been for you and this young man, everything could have been very, very different. I do beg of you, if there is anything I can do to help you, don't hesitate to ask.'

'It's just that …' She broke off again. Beautiful acting. She seemed to be summoning up the courage to tell him. 'It's just that I'm out of a job right now!'

He stared at her thoughtfully, and his blue eyes wrinkled. 'Well, well, well,' he said, with a fatherly air. 'That shouldn't be too difficult to arrange. What kind of work to you do?'

She became suddenly shy, looked down at her dainty feet, flushed charmingly. 'I'm not very much good at anything really, except maybe helping around the house.' She looked up at him quickly. 'Isn't there some way I could help you here?' she asked, anxiously. 'Help nurse you; look after things around the house, help you in little ways?'

Maybe he saw the red light. He lost a lot of his fatherliness, and his voice became bleak. 'Well, I don't know. We have the servants, and everything seems to run along smoothly …'

'There must be something I can do,' she interrupted quickly, anxiously. 'I've had experience in office work. Maybe I could keep your private papers tidy. There's the shopping and ordering groceries. I know about cooking, and it would be a wonderful opportunity for me to get on my feet again. I wouldn't need to live in, unless you wanted, and I feel sure your wife would be only too happy having me around, especially knowing I had helped her.'

The deliberate implication in her last sentence he couldn't ignore.

Greigs drew a deep breath. He didn't like it one little bit, but she was giving him no alternative. 'If you feel so strongly about it, my dear, of course I'll give you a job here until you've got on your feet again.'

'It's so kind of you,' she said, and once again she blushed slyly, lowered her eyelashes, stared down at her dainty feet.

I was glaring at her. I said, brusquely: 'There must be plenty of other places you can work. You can get a job if you want.'

She looked up at me, shot me a vicious glance nobody else saw. Then she said, sweetly: 'I need experience, Hank. That's my real trouble. I can't get a job anywhere without references. And if Mr Greigs finds me satisfactory, I'm sure he'll give me a good reference.'

'Yeah,' I said, hollowly. 'I'm sure he will, if he finds you satisfactory.' There was a sinking feeling in my belly. Because I'd sat beside this dame, heard her ideas on life. I didn't like the smell of this set-up one little bit.

'Can we get you something to eat?' Greigs asked.

'No,' I said quickly. 'Our clothes should be dry now. It's late. We'll be getting along.'

Cora opened her mouth to say something. I grabbed her arm determinedly. 'It's late now, and we don't want to worry you folk. We've got to go right now, so if we decline your invitation, don't think we're being rude.'

'Of course not, Mr Janson,' he said. 'I quite understand. I'll call the butler and see if your clothes are ready.'

'And I start my duties with you tomorrow, Mr Greigs?' asked Cora quickly.

'That's right,' he said, reluctantly. 'You start tomorrow.' There was a note of resignation in his voice.

'I'll have to go home, in any event, then,' she said swiftly. 'I'll have to pack my things.' She looked up at Greigs slyly. 'You will want me to live in, won't you, Mr Greigs?'

He swallowed embarrassedly. 'Yes,' he said, hollowly. 'It would be nice if you would live in.'

4

She sat beside me in the car, wrapped in a shroud of thoughtful silence. I ran down the drive, turned out on the main drag and pointed the bonnet towards Chicago, the city itself.

'Cigarette?' I asked.

'No,' she said, and her voice was a thousand miles away.

'Light me one.'

She sighed, reached for my jacket pocket, pulled out a pack that was a damp, soggy mess of tobacco.

'Try the glove box,' I suggested. 'There should be another packet.'

She found a new pack, lit a cigarette, passed it across with thick red flakes staining the tip.

I drew hard on the cigarette, puffed smoke through my nostrils, said, in a grim voice: 'So you're making a play for the old guy, huh?'

'What's it to you?'

It was a helluva lot to me. The dame had something that got me. Maybe it was jealousy at work deep down inside me. 'Lay off the old fella,' I said.

'You lay off me.'

'He's got dough,' I said. 'He's loaded with it. But he's got a wife too. What do you aim to do, talk him into adopting you?'

'His wife won't live forever.'

I shot her a quick glance. 'She's not all that old. She might even outlive you.'

'She nearly finished herself tonight,' Cora said, quietly. 'Next time she tries, she might be more successful.'

I swerved the car into the side of the road, jammed on the brakes, cut the engine. 'Listen, you little fool,' I snarled. 'D'you realise what you're saying. D'you realise that's crazy talk.'

'Start driving,' she snapped. 'Or do I have to start walking?'

'You sit right there and listen to what I've got to say. D'you understand the crazy thing you're saying? You're waiting for that dame to kick the bucket so you can step into her shoes. You're so damned sure you can get Greigs twisted around your finger, you're ready to stake everything on his wife killing herself.'

'And why not?' she asked, calmly.

I took a deep breath. 'Because it ain't all that easy. Because the set-up ain't clean. Because even if his wife dies naturally, there's gonna be plenty of folk who'll say she got a helping hand. They'll throw a scare into Greigs, point out you've only got one reason for finding a husband old enough to be your grandfather.'

'D'you know something?'

'Tell me.'

'You bore me stiff,' she said, coldly. 'You give me a pain in the neck. You make me sick.'

'You little jerk,' I said, furiously. 'I've a good mind to take you by the shoulders and shake your head off.'

'Get wise, fella,' she snapped. 'One more crack like that and I'll get good and mad.'

'You're set on this?' I asked, grimly. 'You're set on going through with it?'

'Get out of my hair,' she snarled. 'That's all I'm asking. Just keep out of my hair.'

'Okay,' I growled. 'If that's the way you want it, that's the way it's gonna be.' I meant what I said. I was through with her. Because once in a while, a guy has to make a decision about a dame. Either he strings along with her and accepts her the way she is, or he makes a clean break. I started up the engine, let in the clutch, glided away from the kerb.

'Now you're being smart.'

'Lady,' I said, 'this doesn't mean I don't want to take you across my knees, tan your rear until my hand smarts.'

She chuckled, genuinely amused. 'Boy, do you talk big!'

I bit my lip, kept on driving. I drove until we hit the outskirts of Chicago proper.

'Where do you want me to drop you?'

'North side. But if you aren't in the mood for driving, drop me here and I'll get myself a taxi.'

'I'll take you,' I grunted. 'Twenty minutes more won't make much difference.'

It was a more lower-middle class district, a kinda jungle of tenement houses. I stopped outside the house she indicated, turned off the engine.

'Thanks for the buggy ride,' she said.

'I can hardly say it was a pleasure,' I said bitterly.

She bent down, pulled on her shoes.

'D'you live alone?' I asked.

She looked up at me then, her eyes mocking and challenging. 'Let's have it straight, fella,' she said, bluntly. 'What's at the back of your mind?'

'Nothing's at the back of my mind. I just wondered how a dame like you gets by.'

'Come and have a coffee or have a drink. Help yourself to an eyeful. I've nothing to hide.'

'Not now,' I said. 'It's late.'

She raised one eyebrow, grinned derisively. 'Scared, huh?'

I looked at her, stared into those eyes of hers. Slowly I reached for the car key, withdrew it from the socket, put it in my pocket. 'I'll take you up on it,' I said. 'I'll have coffee.'

The stairs were uncarpeted and unlighted. We stumbled our way up four flights of stairs before she asked for a light. I used my cigarette lighter, and in the guttering flame saw her fumbling above the door ledge. She found the key, inserted it in the lock and opened up. She switched on the light, and I followed through into the room.

It was just one room, the kinda room you'd expect a girl like her to have. An iron framed bed was in one corner, rumpled and unmade, the sink in another corner, and alongside it a primus stove. The rest of the furniture was simple and inexpensive. A line strung across the room was draped with damp stockings and underclothing, and everywhere was evidence of dilatoriness.

'D'you know how to light a primus stove?' she asked.

'Maybe you want I should make the coffee?' I sneered.

'Light the stove and put on the kettle. I'll do the rest.'

I found the kettle, blackened from paraffin smoke. I filled it with water, placed it on the primus, used mentholated spirits to get the primus stove flaring, and pumped hard. That took maybe all of five minutes. When I turned around to see what she was doing, she had her back towards me. She was bare to the waist, pulling over her head a newly laundered blouse. Seeing the soft brownness of her back reminded me of how I'd seen her earlier. She'd got me sweating then, made me stare like I was hypnotised. And now, as though she could feel my hot eyes fastened to her, she swung around, stared at me with that damnable, mocking, indulgent smile curling her lips, her eyes dancing with devilment.

'I've put on the kettle,' I said, hoarsely.

'You were watching me,' she accused.

'Sure I was watching. Do you blame me?'

'You're a real fall guy, aren't you?' she mocked. 'You go for me, don't you? You hate yourself like hell for it, but you can't stop yourself, can you?'

'You're wasting your time,' I growled. 'I ain't got no dough. I'm just a reporter. Reporters don't make fortunes.'

'But you like watching me, huh?' She was still smiling mockingly, moved in a pace towards me, her teeth white and gleaming, eyes dancing and somehow making me acutely conscious she was wearing nothing beneath that slim, crisp, freshly laundered blouse.

'Why the hell did I have to meet you?' I complained.

'It's life,' she said. 'These things happen.' She was hovering in front of me, mocking me, challenging me, almost daring me.

'Listen,' I pleaded, urgently. 'Lay off that old guy, will ya? You're too smart a dame to get tied up in that kind of mess.'

'Think you can persuade me to lay off?' Her voice was unadulterated mockery, and she was an irresistible tantalisation.

I hardly knew I was doing it. I moved in towards her, my mind a hot whirl. I was rough with her, grabbed her tightly. Her body was hard against mine, and her soft, mocking chuckle floated on the air a few moments before I rammed my lips hard against hers.

Her lips responded, hot, moist and open, her skin hot beneath the thin blouse. Her arms were strong and urging as she yielded to me, moulded herself against me, abandoned herself in an embrace that was complete surrender.

It left me breathless. I pulled my lips away from hers with a kind of sob, brushed them down across her cheek to the nape of her neck.

She quivered deliriously, held me even more tightly. And she wasn't playing. She was as hot as me. Maybe hotter. Her thighs were rammed so hard against me they hurt, and her fingers were feverish and frantic. The skin of her throat was tantalisingly cool beneath my lips, the smell of her perfume strong in my nostrils, intoxicating and heady. Her breath was hot on my neck, and she was panting. Then we were grasping at each other so wildly, we swayed, almost lost balance.

Her fingers were pressing hard on my face, turning it towards hers. 'Kiss me,' she panted. 'Kiss me that way again.' There was a savage intensity in her voice.

Her lips were open, hot, burning and moist. There was a searing, expanding flame inside me that her hot lips were drawing out of me, hot blood was pulsing through my brain with a confusing intensity, and somehow we were against the bed so that it hit our thighs, caused us to topple, sprawl on it, locked together in a fierce embrace.

It was a crazy, savage embrace. My lips, fingers and body were bruising her at the same time. And she wanted to be bruised; abandoned herself completely to the savageness of desire.

Then quite suddenly it was totally different. She stopped fighting, became still and rigid, her hands suddenly losing sensitivity, her lips warm but no longer searching. It was like applying the brakes strongly when you're full out.

Emotionally it was terrifying, like I'd been floating on a magic carpet, deliriously happy, and then suddenly discovered that the carpet had vanished, that I was falling, falling like a stone, down and down into a yawning black abyss.

'What is it?' I croaked. 'What's the matter?'

She didn't reply for a few seconds. It was like she was recovering her breath. 'This is it, fella,' she said. 'This is the end of the line. We don t go any further.'

Her body was hot and throbbing, her skin burning beneath that thin blouse. 'What's biting you, honey? I whispered. 'I do something wrong?'

'Fella. You ain't done nothing at all. Nothing at all. That's the way I want it to be.'

Every second, she was becoming more and more remote, kinda drawing away from me and into herself, aloof mentally and physically so that I couldn't touch her.

'You've got me gunning for you,' I said, hotly.

She hunched one shoulder irritably. 'Quit doing that,' she snapped.

'Isn't it what you want?'

She hunched her shoulder again, pushed at me with her hand. 'It's not what I want. It's just … irritating.'

'If it isn't pleasant now, it will be … soon.' My voice was thick, heavy with desire.

She squirmed away from me, traced a bleeding, painful pattern on my back with her sharp nails. 'Didn't you hear me?' she said, harshly. 'I said cut it out.'

She meant it.

I was hot; as hot as hell. I wanted her so badly I couldn't think clearly. And she was right beside me, hot and throbbing, alive and vital. And despite my better judgment, I became persistent, tried to fan into flame the slumbering fire inside her.

Her voice was grating and ugly. 'Listen, you big dope,' she snarled. 'Are you gonna cut it out or am I gonna have to get rough?' As she spoke, she raised one threatening, claw-tipped hand, rested it gently against my cheek, one sharply pointed nail pricking my eyelid, ready to slash and tear. Her voice left no doubt she meant every word she said.

I was quite still, fighting hard to control the hunger inside me.

She growled with exasperation. 'What a weight you are!'

I was still breathing heavily, but I had myself under control now. 'Why d'you start this?' I demanded, thickly. 'What are you playing at?'

'Listen, dope,' she gritted. 'If you want a philosophical discussion, find yourself a chair to park on. There's a coupla ways I know to show I ain't happy this way. D'you want I should use them?'

'I get it,' I said, breathing heavily. 'You were playing with me.'

'Sure, that's right,' she grunted. 'Now, move over, willya?'

'Just practising, huh?'

'That's the idea. Gee, that's better.' She breathed with relief, pushed herself into a sitting position, straightened out her blouse, buttoned up the lower buttons.

'D'you get a kick outta making a sucker of a guy?' I demanded angrily.

Her eyes were full of amused mockery. 'I've been good to you, fella. I've been teaching you something. I warned you that you were easy. I said any dame could make you turn somersaults. Now I've proved it for you.'

'Not just any dame,' I said, thickly.

She looked at me shrewdly, narrowed her eyes. 'Something special about me, huh?'

'Yeah,' I said, hotly, 'something special about *you*,' and I leaned towards her.

She caught my hand expertly, gouged nails deep into my flesh. Her eyes were angry, scornful and contemptuous. 'Cut it out,' she snarled, wearily. 'Are you so dumb you can't understand? I don't play that way. I don't play for keeps. This is the end of the line, Bud. Can't you get that into your head?'

I got to my feet slowly. It took an effort, but I made it. I stood looking down at her and she looked up at me, her mouth quirked in that half-cynical, half-mocking smile.

'Okay,' I growled. 'So you've made a monkey out of me. That's what you wanted, isn't it? You wanted to prove you could get me going.'

She chuckled. A low, deep chuckle. 'I wanted you to get wise to yourself. I told you you're a pushover. Now maybe you'll believe it for yourself.'

'I guess you get a kick out of it,' I said, bitterly. 'It makes you feel good, makes you feel you have the whole world at your feet.'

'Yeah,' she agreed, mockingly. 'That's just the way I feel.' She got to her feet, finished buttoning her blouse. All I had left in me was a glare. I gave her the full benefit of it, turned on my heel and made towards the door.

'Hey,' she called. 'How about the coffee?'

'You drink it,' I said. 'I don't need anything to keep me awake. I'm going to have a sleepless night anyway.'

I was hoping she'd come after me, head me off, take me by the arm and apologise for having strung me along too far. But she didn't.

I reached the door, turned the door handle, hesitated, waited for some sign of her weakening.

She said coolly, mockingly: 'Good night. And please don't slam the door as you leave.'

I climbed into my car, and I was still hot. I sat there for maybe five minutes, simmering with the anger of frustration, telling myself what a dope I was to fall for a dame like her. My fingers were shaking when I turned the key in the dashboard, started the engine and headed towards my apartment.

Dawn was breaking when I arrived. I didn't bother to put the car in the garage, I parked it out front in the parking lot. It had been a long night, and I was tired. I wearily climbed the stairs to my apartment, because the bell hop was snoring on his tip-up seat, opened the door of my apartment and sidled inside.

She was there in the living room, curled up on the settee with her red hair splayed across the cushions, her dainty shoes kicked off and the table lamp burning.

I crept past her into the bedroom, further on into the bathroom. I was tired now. Very tired. Living in a kinda unreal world. I wasn't gonna get a chance to make up the sleep I'd lost, so I stripped off, stepped under the shower, pelted my hide with hot water until I was hard boiled. Then I switched over to ice-cold.

I came out of that shower with my body glowing, but my head heavy, and my eyes tired. I had the uncomfortable sensation that tiny particles of sand were embedded in the back of my eyeballs, irritating and painful. I reached for my pants, and she said from the doorway: 'You're too big a boy to be running around that way.'

I kept my shoulders towards her, climbed into my pants hurriedly. 'Hiya, Scallywag,' I said uneasily.

'That's better,' she said approvingly. 'Much better, much better for my peace of mind. You make a girl nervous, running around that way.'

I turned to face her, grinned uneasily and reached for my shirt. She was smiling sweetly, but I recognised the anger signs. Her rich red hair was dishevelled, her frock creased, and tiny red glints gleamed deep down in her green eyes. Yeah, she was mad. And pretty soon, the storm was gonna break.

'I'm sorry I'm late,' I said lamely.

'It's nothing, nothing at all,' she said airily. 'I just love sitting around for hours waiting. It's the thing I do best of all, the thing I've had most practice at.'

'I'll tell you the way it was …' I began.

'I know,' she cut in. 'You warned me you were going to be late, asked me to wait for you.' She glanced towards the window. The grey of daylight was becoming brighter, the soft morning noises of an awakening world growing stronger. 'Maybe you figure five or six hours waiting isn't so long.'

'Listen, Scallywag, I'll tell you just the way it was. I'd have been here at once, maybe half-past one, if it hadn't been for this dame who jumped in the river. I was the only person around to see her do it. I just had to do something about it and ...'

'Sure, I understand,' she said mockingly. 'You've spent the last five hours swimming up and down the river.'

My dried clothes were soiled, rumpled and badly in need of cleaning and pressing. I crossed to my wardrobe, opened it up, pulled out another suit. 'You figure I'm spinning a line,' I growled angrily. 'You figure I'm faking an explanation.'

'Listen, you big ape,' she said softly, the first hint of the lash of her tongue. 'You don't have to give me explanations. But if you do, make them good.'

I said slowly, dangerously calm. 'The dame jumped in the river, see. I fished her out. I took her home. I dried off my clothes there and it took time. And if you think I'm kidding, take a look at my suit. It's still damp.'

Her green eyes stared into mine, and suddenly she was incredibly attractive, her red hair a flaming halo that made her soft skin seem even softer. 'Okay, Hank,' she said quietly. 'I believe you.' Yet just the same she crossed the room, picked up my jacket, fingered it to test the dampness.

'I'm sorry, Sheila,' I said sincerely. 'I wanted to be back on time to meet you. Honest.'

She was still holding my jacket. She said softly, wistfully. 'We were gonna have an evening together, Hank, remember? It's been a long while. It took a lot of angling to fix tonight.' She shrugged her shoulders ruefully. 'And now the opportunity's been lost.'

I knew the way she was feeling. Both of us working on the *Chronicle* on different assignments kept us apart. The last half dozen times we'd arranged to spend a few hours together, one or other of us had been called out on a story. We'd figured in the early hours of the morning we'd get a chance to spend a little time together without interruption.

But that damned woman had spoiled everything with a header into the river.

'Listen, Sheila,' I said sincerely. 'We're gonna fix it good this time. We're gonna fix an appointment that nothing's gonna stop. Next time, I'm gonna keep the appointment for sure. Even if the *Chronicle* goes bust on account of it, I'll keep the appointment. What do you say, kid? Any time, any place. Just tell me, and I'll make it.'

She was still holding my jacket. She moved over towards me. 'You're cute, Hank,' she said, with a soft, mocking note in her voice.

She was melting me. She always had that effect upon me. I seemed to lose some of my tiredness, the pricking at the back of my eyes became less pronounced.

'I've missed you, kid,' I said, and I was a little breathless.

She'd moved right close to me now, gazed into my yes tenderly, still clutching my jacket. 'I've missed you, too, Hank,' she said, and there was a soft note in her voice that puzzled me, a note that was just a little too sweet, a little too tender.

'You're still mad at me, Sheila,' I guessed. 'Even though I've explained everything, you're still mad at me. But listen, kid, I couldn't help it, really.'

'No, Hank,' she purred, 'you couldn't help it,' and she was kinda leaning towards me, her dishevelled hair falling across her forehead, tantalising me, her warm, red lips kinda half-open and expectant.

'Gee, you're cute,' I said breathlessly.

'You're cute too,' she whispered, and leaned even more towards me.

I couldn't resist her. I'd never been able to. I reached out for her, wanted to crush her against me and feel the warmth and vital strength of her throbbing through me. Then, as I moved, she erupted into volcanic, tempestuous fury.

She was small, neat, perfectly proportioned and as feminine as any guy could want a dame to be. But she could be tough too. Damned tough. She had to be. She was a newspaper woman, and when she was mad, she was a small but dynamic explosion of human emotion.

It was so unexpected that I didn't even see her small, hard fist as it uppercutted with all the pent-up anger flaming inside her. Small, hard knuckles exploded against my jaw, jerking my head backwards. Another clenched fist buried itself in my solar plexus with breathtaking agony. A rain of blows flailed my head, face and chest so that I staggered backwards, caught my heel against a chair, tripped and sat heavily on the floor.

I shook my head to clear it, stared up at her through a mist of bewilderment.

And was she angry.

She was as angry as I'd ever seen her.

She was flaming mad!

Her green eyes were hard and cutting, slashing my soul into strips that could be hung up and dried. Her red hair was a flaming denunciation, her heaving breasts, an indignant, exasperated accusation, and her clenched fists at her sides, showed how much self-control she was exerting to prevent herself tearing at me with teeth and nails.

'Hey,' I gasped. 'What's the idea? What's this all about?'

'I'm cute, aren't I?' she gritted, and the bitterness of her voice cut into me. 'You like me one hell of a lot. You'd do anything for me,' she grated furiously.

'Sure, kid,' I said, getting one hand underneath me so I could climb to my feet.

'And the woman you saved from drowning. Just what was she drowning in?' she demanded furiously.

'Listen, kid …' I began.

She stopped, picked up my jacket. Her eyes lashed at me with a contemptuous, scornful glare that hurt. Hurt, because Sheila meant more to me than she knew.

'Don't bother to see me out,' she snarled. 'And don't bother to speak to me again.' There was bitter hurt in her eyes, too, as she flung my jacket straight in my face. It hit me as I was climbing to my feet, toppled me off balance so that I fell back on the floor with it wrapped around my head.

I clawed the jacket from my face, heard the door of my flat slam. I made a quick movement to get to my feet and go after her. But it would be useless. I sank back on the floor dejectedly. What the hell had gotten into her, anyway?

And then I got it myself. With the jacket still draped round my shoulders, I couldn't help getting it.

Mrs Greigs wasn't the only one who had tried to drown herself. Cora had tried too. But Cora had used scent instead of water.

And that scent was clinging to my jacket like wallpaper to the wall.

5

What can a guy do at six o'clock in the morning when it's too late to go to bed and too early to go to the office? I went through to the kitchen, made myself coffee, thick and black. I kept thinking about Sheila, what a grand kid she was and how bad things musta looked to her.

Then I started in thinking about Cora, remembering her cocky pertness, her lopsided view of life, the stark materialism of her approach to human relationships. Then I was remembering her eyes, the way they seemed to open wide a door on her personality, a personality so feminine and magnetic it got a hold on me, made me weak inside, like my bones were jelly and my will-power flabby and easily moulded into any shape she fancied.

It was a bitter memory.

She'd played with me, taunted me, strung along with me, and finally, with the dexterity and skill of a specialist, she'd switched me over from hot to cold, contemptuous and mocking at my weakness.

Yeah, she had made a fool of me. Showed me the way she could get a guy panting on the top line and then switch off the magic.

She was right. I'd been taught a lesson.

But I hadn't learned anything by it. Because right then, while thinking about her, I forgot Sheila, forgot the other dames I knew, found myself thinking about Cora and wanting her.

Wanting that pert, cheeky-faced, hard-as-nails materialist in skirts.

What was so special about this one dame? She hadn't tried to spin me a line. She'd put her cards on the table. She was out for money, the big money. And to get it, she frankly admitted she was prepared to use every and any angle possible. She'd played with me, toyed with my emotions like an expert pianist dashing off a prelude with experienced ease and perfection. And I didn't mean a thing to her. She'd made that quite clear, and I knew it. I knew it as surely as I knew my name was Janson.

But I still wanted her.

I looked up her name in the telephone book. But it wasn't there. That type of room in a tenement house wouldn't have a phone. There'd be one phone for the whole house, and that would be rented in the name of the landlady.

But I did know her address!

I toyed with the idea of going round to see her. But I knew the way it would be. She'd open up, sleepy-eyed, unwashed and flaming mad. She'd tell me to get the hell out of it so she could sleep. Then, crushed and humbled, I'd have to leave her, wishing I'd never thought of calling.

It was better not to see her ever again, I decided. Better to forget her.

It was a decision easy to make but difficult to fulfil.

I poured myself a Scotch, drank it slowly, relished the raw bite of it on my tongue and the warm glow it spread inside my stomach. I was tired now, my head heavy and my eyes set in sandpaper sockets.

But there was no chance I could sleep.

I walked halfway to the office, found a snack bar open with the first early morning customers seated at the counter. I climbed on to a high stool, ordered myself a helping of ham and eggs and coffee, borrowed a copy of the morning paper, and whiled away the time until I was due in at the office.

It was one of those grey days when nothing seems to go right. Moreover, I had a persistent hangover from a sleepless night, the grittiness at the back of my eyes becoming more and more pronounced every hour.

I was the first to arrive in the office, and on my desk was the biggest pile of correspondence I've ever seen. I looked at it glumly, started sorting through it, dropping into the wastepaper basket the letters that didn't need to be answered, sending through to the Investigation Department information that had been volunteered and that needed checking, and keeping on one side those rare but useful letters, usually anonymous, that gave genuine inside information.

The newsroom began to fill. By ten o'clock, the telephones were jangling, shirt-sleeved, sweating reporters were banging away at typewriters, messengers were scurrying back and fro to the print room and my head was heavy on my shoulders, like a leaden football.

Conway, the sports reporter, lounged over to my desk, looked at me sympathetically. 'Looks like a bad case of haemorrhage,' he said.

'What does?' I growled.

'Finest case of bloodshot eyes I've ever seen. What happened? Did she fight back at you all night?'

It was intended as a joke, but it was so near the truth, it hurt. 'Find yourself a nice bag,' I said bitterly. 'Put your head in it and come back. I'll pull the cords tight.'

'Feeling good and tough, huh?' he grinned.

'Sure,' I said grimly. 'That's the way I feel. Wanna make something of it?'

'Listen, fella,' he said, not grinning any longer. 'It's you that needs the bag. An ice bag. Why start on me? Can I help it if your eyes weep blood?'

My head was so heavy, it needed all my strength to prevent it falling forward on the table. 'Scram,' I said wearily. 'Leave me alone, will ya? Peddle your wisecracks elsewhere.'

He stared at me strangely, shrugged his shoulders, went back to his own desk. I knew I was behaving badly, but the way I felt, I just couldn't help myself. That's the way it gets you when you lose sleep.

I felt bad, lifeless and leaden. What I wanted was to go

home, take off my shoes, lie on the bed, and drift off into blissful slumber. But the *Chicago Chronicle* doesn't pay wages to guys so they can stretch out on a bed in stockinged feet.

It was at half-past ten when I got the call. The operator said: 'There's a guy on the phone who won't give his name. Says he must speak to you. Says it's most important, a matter of life or death.'

'Okay, put him through,' I said wearily.

The voice was deep, obviously disguised and impregnated with a conspiratorial note that got me interested.

'Am I speaking to Hank Janson?'

'Sure,' I said. 'What do you want?'

'How do I know it's Hank Janson?'

'What d'you want I should do? Show you my birthmarks?'

'Listen,' he said urgently. 'This is serious. It's a matter of life or death. There can't be a slip-up. Hank Janson's the only guy who can handle this. Put me through to him, will you?'

'Drop the cloak and dagger line,' I grated. 'This is Hank Janson. Who the devil are you?'

There was silence, a long silence. Then he said, cautiously: 'I've got to be sure.'

'Come round to the office,' I suggested.

'I've got a better idea. You meet me some place. I'll recognise you.'

'You meet me here.'

'Too risky,' he said with finality.

'Okay. Think it over. Ring me back when you've changed your mind.'

He said quickly: 'If you really are Janson, you'd better be smart. The kinda information I've got is hot. So hot, I ain't talking to anyone but Hank Janson. This thing's so hot, if it gets out I've talked, I'm a cold turkey.'

'Why are you talking, then?' I demanded suspiciously.

His voice was loaded with hatred. 'Because there's a guy I've got to get even with.'

'So you wanna squeal, huh?' I demanded. 'You wanna give me the low-down on someone. So, why ring me? Why not ring police headquarters?'

His voice was harsh and irritated. 'Listen, Buster,' he growled. 'D'you wanna story that's gonna lift the roof off Chicago, or don't you? If you do, you're playing it the wrong way. You're playing it like a sucker. I'm handing you a story on a plate, a red-hot story that's sizzling. D'you think I'm going to walk into police headquarters and tell them what I know?'

'Depends on what it is you know.'

'Listen, jerk,' he snarled. 'You give me a pain in the neck. D'you want this story or don't you?'

He was keen to feed me the information, and if my head hadn't been as heavy as lead, I'd have been as keen to get it. 'Okay,' I said wearily. 'What d'you want I should do?'

'D'you know Max Keller's bar?'

'Sure,' I protested. 'But that's right out on North Side.'

'There's a small snack bar just opposite, further along. Johnny's cafe. Meet you there in half-an-hour.'

'Wait a minute,' I protested. 'Make it someplace handy. That's a long way.'

'Remember it, Buster,' he said. 'Johnny's cafe. Just opposite Max Keller's bar. I'll meet you there in half-an-hour.' He wasn't arguing any longer. He hung up.

I looked at my watch. I calculated it would take me twenty minutes driving hard. My eyes were still gritty, my head even heavier, and the effort of getting up from my desk made me feel even weaker, like my head was seventeen times its normal size.

I slumped down at my desk again. It was a relief just sitting and holding my head in my hands. Why the hell did I need to chase over to North Side anyway? Okay, so there was a chance of a story. But I'd handled plenty of stories in my time. Too many! What could be so special about this?

I sat there with my head aching and my limbs heavy and tired. Yet the conspiratorial note in his voice kept echoing in my mind; the mysterious urgency of his voice and his insistence he should speak only to me produced a quickening surge of interest.

I didn't wanna go. My body was howling a protest as I

reached down into my desk drawer, pulled out a bottle of rye I kept for emergencies.

I took a good pull, felt the raw spirit burn my mouth and tongue, rolled it around my teeth and let it trickle down my throat. It was strong stuff, that; good, strong rye that had been smuggled through the customs from Canada. It spread out inside my chest like the sun radiating heat.

I straightened up, drew the back of my hand across my lips, put the bottle back in the drawer, and caught Conway eyeing me speculatively. 'Hair of the dog, huh?' he said across the room.

I scowled.

He grinned.

I got up, felt my legs rubbery beneath me. I took a deep breath and a grip on myself, strode determinedly to the hat stand, crushed my fedora on my head and made for the exit.

I located Max Keller's bar easily enough. And as he had said, a few doors along the street on the other side, I found Johnny's cafe.

I drove past it slowly, scrutinised it carefully from the outside. It was just one of a thousand cafes you can find in Chicago.

I parked my car further along the street, climbed out from it slowly, locked it with my car key, deliberately selected a cigarette from my pack and lit up slowly. All the time, my eyes were busy, scrutinising the passers-by, searching for a familiar face and trying to decide who, if any, was the mysterious man who had telephoned.

I didn't see anyone who looked like he was looking for me. All I earned myself was a reminder of the sand grinding at the back of my eyes.

I paused again at the entrance to Joe's cafe, glanced up and down the street. There was nobody paying me especial attention. I glanced at my wristwatch, saw I was five minutes ahead of time. I sighed, mentally shrugged my shoulders, pushed my way inside.

It was a small cafe and crowded; not a vacant seat available.

It was the wrong type of place and the wrong time to meet anyone. If the guy had secret information to give me, we'd have to use the deaf and dumb language. The customers were mainly office workers taking their mid-morning coffee. In a few minutes, they'd probably be leaving. Maybe he was counting on that.

To fill in time, I crossed to the kiosk, locked myself inside, rang the *Chicago Chronicle* and asked for the Information Department.

The Information Department was a new innovation at the *Chronicle*, devised for the purpose of saving reporters' leg work.

'That you, Slim?' I asked.

'Oh, it's you,' he grunted disagreeably. 'Isn't there anything you find out for yourself?'

'Sure,' I said. 'And what I find out gets printed. What you find out helps fill in the picture.'

'Okay, go ahead,' he growled wearily. 'I've got my pencil ready.'

'Dig up all you can on a guy named Greigs. He's an old guy, maybe sixty-five. Lives out on Northumberland Avenue. Got a big house there that must be worth plenty of dough. Get me his pedigree, his bank account and anything else you can ferret out.'

'I'll even let you know what size boots he wears.'

When I quit the telephone kiosk, there was one vacant seat at a small table. I sat down, and the girl sitting opposite looked away from me with a disdainful air.

I looked at her.

She acted like I wasn't there.

I kept on looking at her.

She drew hard on her cigarette, stared over her empty coffee cup and across my shoulder like I had no existence.

I kept on looking at her.

She drew on her cigarette again, hurriedly this time. Too hurriedly! She was getting nervous.

'You don't mind me sitting here?' I asked politely.

With an effort she drew her eyes to mine. They were nice

eyes. And she was a nice kid. Maybe twenty-three. She had a cheerful face and a cheeky upturned nose. Trying to be disdainful and aloof wasn't in her line. But she tried it.

'I beg your pardon?' she said coldly, her tone saying, '*How dare you speak to me.*'

'I asked if you objected to my sitting here.'

'Object? Why should I object?' she asked coldly, distantly.

'On account you're acting like I'm a bad smell.'

'I beg your pardon,' she said haughtily. 'I wasn't aware I was inhaling in an unusual manner.'

'Well, how about a little smile, huh?'

Her eyes stared coldly, widened, switched to my right shoulder. 'I don't smile at strangers.' she stated icily.

The counter jerk was hovering beside me now. 'What d'you want, Bud?' he demanded. He was sweating, beads of moisture trickling down the unhealthy, whitish pallor of his forehead.

'I'll take a coffee,' I told him.

'What about you, lady?'

'Sure,' I said. 'She'll take a coffee, too. Won't you?'

She looked at me, she looked at the counter jerk, and for seconds that seemed minutes, she waged an internal war.

All at once she capitulated. 'Okay,' she sighed. 'I guess I'll take another coffee.'

'It's my invitation,' I said.

'Sure it won't break you?'

'Listen,' I said. 'Loosen up. Smile. Melt. Be human. Don't give the world the cold shoulder. Life's too short. We only kick around on this world for an average of three score and ten. And a third of that time we spend sleeping. You wanna be as happy and as sociable as possible while you can. You know how the minutes fly and the weeks pass like lightning. In no time, a month has slipped past. Twelve months make a year. The years slip past without you noticing, and before you know where you are, bingo! You're wondering what you've been doing all your life.'

She smiled a little. 'What are you trying to do? Prepare me for my old age pension?'

'That's better,' I said. 'Now you're melting.'

Her eyes flashed dangerously. 'Don't get the wrong idea. I'm talking, that's all. I'm not used to allowing fellas to make me.'

'Do I act like I'm making you?'

She pouted. 'I guess not.' Then she added, warningly: 'But just don't start. That's all. I've got a fella I'm engaged to and …'

'And he'll tear my arm off, beat me to death with it,' I put in.

She grinned ruefully as she looked me over.

'Well, I guess he'd try, anyway.'

'Getting married soon?' I asked.

'Monday week.'

'Gonna have a big family?'

'Dozens of kids,' she said, and her eyes were sparkling as she thought of the future.

The perspiring counter jerk smeared his napkin across the marble-topped table, banged down two coffees, which were overflowing into the saucers. Almost before the cups had touched down, he was speeding towards the other end of the cafe to take fresh orders.

'I guess I was wrong,' she admitted. 'You're a sociable guy. You're not a shark.'

I was watching everyone in the cafe carefully, searching for the man who might own the voice I'd heard over the telephone. It was a few minutes after eleven now, and I was regretting having come. I felt in my bones that this was a bum steer, that I'd made a wasted journey. I've had dozens of hoax calls in my time, but I've only been caught out once or twice. This time, I hadn't been up to my usual standard of alertness, on account of my heavy head and smarting eyes.

'I thought you were just on the make,' she said.

I drew my eyes back to hers. 'Maybe I was, kid,' I admitted absently. 'But then I didn't know about the boyfriend, did I?'

'Lost interest now?'

'We can still be pals.'

She grinned, showed clean, white teeth. I fumbled in my pocket, offered her my cigarette case. She puffed hard on the cigarette and blew smoke into my face. She did it with a kinda mocking, challenging smile.

'What's your age, kid?'

'Twenty-three.'

'Quite a baby.'

She puckered her forehead in a mock frown. 'The way you talk, anyone would think you old enough to be my father.'

'Maybe I am,' I said bitterly. 'Maybe I've lived enough to be ten times my age.' I was thinking of the misery, drama and vice I'd seen while I'd been a reporter. I'd rubbed shoulders with life at its worst, found myself time and again precipitated into experiences that no man should encounter more than once in a lifetime.

'Maybe I'm a hundred years old,' I said.

Her eyes were wide, youthful and puzzled. 'You talk strangely.'

'Yeah,' I said. 'I talk – I talk because of what I am. I'm words. A factory of words. I'm made of words. They bubble out of me – a never-ending river of words.'

There was the slightest hint of alarm in her eyes now. She said hurriedly: 'I'd better be going. I'm late.' She sipped at her coffee.

I chuckled. 'You think I'm crazy, huh?'

Her eyes were earnest, watchful and yet curious. 'I think you're different,' she said. 'Different from most other men I know.'

'Sure I'm different,' I said. 'I breakfast with murder and hatred, who are twins. I take lunch with vice and bestiality, I sip tea with accidental death and eat dinner cheek by jowl with chaos, destruction and misery.'

She stared, wide-eyed.

'You don't know what the hell I'm talking about, do you?'

She shook her head, dumbly.

'Just as well, kid,' I said kindly. 'Drink your coffee. Go back to your office. Go to church Monday week and later have dozens of kids. Better still, have hundreds of kids. The more you have, the more chance some will get through.'

'D'you always talk this way?'

'Nope,' I said. 'Usually I stick to philosophical treatise, confine myself to the Socratic dialectical method of conversation.'

'Whew,' she breathed. 'The words you use!'

My guess had been right. The customers were filing out now, going back to their offices.

She said: 'Is there someone you're looking for?'

'Just a friend,' I said casually, 'just a friend,' and sipped my coffee.

It was terrible coffee.

'I'm overdue at the office,' she told me. But she made no attempt to leave.

'What does your boyfriend do for a living?'

The cafe was deserted now, except for a thin, weary-looking, middle-aged guy who sat hunched over an empty coffee cup. He didn't look the sort of guy who would make that telephone call. He didn't even look as though he had the strength to telephone.

'Fred hasn't a very good job at the moment,' she told me. 'He's just a truck driver. But he's studying awful hard. That's why we haven't seen much of each other.'

I looked at my watch. It was ten minutes past the scheduled time. I'd been played for a sucker. I'd wasted my time following a blind lead.

'I'll walk you back to your office,' I told her.

'Oh, no, please don't do that,' she said quickly, just a little scared. She broke off, paused, added in a controlled voice: 'It isn't really necessary. Please don't bother.'

I wasn't looking at her. I was looking over her shoulder at the swing doors. There were just four of us in the cafe now. The thin, weary guy drooping over his empty cup, the counter jerk, the dame and me. And the guy peering through the glass swing doors looked just the kinda guy who might have made that telephone call. Burly, broad-shouldered, black fedora pulled well down over his forehead, white, flabby cheeks and coal black eyes.

He saw me. He recognised me. He pushed in through the

swing doors, came to a standstill just inside, stared at me levelly with both hands rammed deep down in the pockets of his grey slicker. I stared back at him and saw the hatred in his black eyes, a bitter, distrustful hatred that got all my nerves jangling, stretched to tension point.

From the corner of my eye, I saw the weary guy fumbling in his pocket for a cigarette. The counter jerk had his head down below the counter washing a dirty cup. The dame was staring at me, waiting for me to insist on accompanying her to her office.

And me?

I was staring at the guy, with the hairs prickling on the nape of my neck, some unsuspected mental danger signal sounding an alarm inside me. It was instinct – just instinct. I'd never seen the guy before, didn't know who he was or what he wanted. But those black eyes were a menace in themselves. A menace that was half-numbing.

That was when I regretted the heaviness of my head, the soreness of my eyes and the fatigue of my body. Because suddenly everything was tension, everything necessitated action.

I saw the menace in his eyes as his arm flexed to move, sensed his finger crooked around the trigger as he drew the gun from his pocket. I read in his eyes the deadly determination to kill, to pump lead at me until the gun was empty and I was riddled with bullets.

His action was the spasmodic burst of a concealed machine gun springing into life, erupting leaden death. And it was concentrated action, minutes cramped into seconds, movements concertinaed into flickers.

In such moments, you don't consciously think, you act.

I had three thoughts in my mind. To get the dame out of danger, to get myself out of immediate danger and to get my hands on that guy, choke the life out of him.

My movements were synchronised. As his hand emerged from his pocket, revealing the grim glint of steel, I was lunging across the table, sweeping her to one side so that she fell to the right, the chair skeltering away across the floor. Then my fingers were hooking over the rim of the marble-topped table and I was launching myself backwards, pulling the table with me, pulling it up and over me so it formed a natural shield between me and the lead that would spurt.

I was falling back now, my chair kicked away from beneath me, the table a heavy weight that was threatening to fall too far, topple over on top of me. I gripped the table hard, gritted my teeth, braced myself as my shoulders hit the floor. And as the table teetered off balance, it vibrated beneath the impact of lead. I heard ricocheting lead scream around the café, and gunfire echoed deafeningly in that confined space. My hands were burning, stung by the vibration of marble as it splintered beneath the impact of lead. And I was flaming mad, mad that I should have been caught in such a trap, furious that a guy should try to make a sitting duck of me, half-crazed with anger, fear and shock.

Yet subconsciously my mind was working like lightning. He'd fired three shots. It meant he still had three left, and my hand was reaching, grasping my chair, every action instinctive and automatic.

I hurled the chair without seeing him, skimmed it across the marble top as I lay there with my shoulders on the floor. It caught him as he was running in at me, caught him with the revolver half-raised to fire again, smashed against his upraised forearm, sent him staggering backwards.

Then without thinking I was on my toes, launching myself across the table-top, diving at him in a body tackle that I couldn't stop and he couldn't dodge. Just before I hit him, the half-raised revolver spat twice, flame seared my eyeballs, smoke caused my throat and nose to sting, lead whistled past me, seared my side like a branding iron.

And then I hit him.

He'd been counting on a sitting duck. He hadn't bargained on counter-action. We hit the floor together hard. Me on top! I had my knee in his groin and my fingers wrapped around his throat, all set to kill him, choke the life out of him, a blind red haze of rage engulfing me.

But my subconscious was still working. Five bullets. That meant one more bullet to come. My fingers left his throat, went for his gun hand. I felt his wrist jump as I wrenched, and the last slug hissed past my ear, smashed into the ceiling above us. I went for his throat again, buried my thumbs deep, gouged and dug with my thumbs like I wanted to pluck out his windpipe.

And that was where I went wrong.

I should have remembered a gun can do more than fire slugs.

I sensed the gun-butt swishing down towards me, swayed my head to one side and gasped with pain as metal split my skull, saw stars shooting across my eyeballs. Blindly, vaguely, I groped for his gun-hand, caught his wrist, found myself clutching nothing as he wrenched free. The next time he struck, the downswing was unavoidable.

Pain seared through my skull, a blackness shot with fiery sparks enveloped my brain. My body, arms and legs were enveloped in thick treacle, and a sensation of falling made my stomach turn somersaults.

I was falling, falling, falling, waiting for the impact of my body against concrete, an impact that would reduce me to a red smear. And all the time I was falling, the cloud of blackness was rolling around me, hugging me tight, weighing me down like a leaden shroud.

Slowly the falling diminished, until I was floating, floating in a world of pain-impregnated blackness, floating yet feeling the hardness of the ground pressing hard and painfully against the back of my head and against my shoulders.

There were voices, too. Loud, urgent, clamouring voices. There was cold moisture on my forehead, an insistent voice compelling my attention; hard pressure against my lips that hurt, forcing me to open my mouth, and china clinking against my teeth as burning liquid ran into my mouth.

Painfully I opened my eyes, saw blurred faces staring down at me, felt my body floating in a sea of pain as though tethered to my head by a slender cord. The voices were still talking, still urging me, and the cool softness of a wet cloth was against my forehead, dabbing the sore, pained swelling that was my head.

'How d'you feel, Buster?'

'He's coming round now!'

'The doctor'll be here soon.'

'He's not hurt that bad, just stunned.'

I was beginning to get the faces into focus, beginning to remember things, too. I made an effort, managed to sit up while helping hands supported me.

'Where is he?' I croaked. 'What happened to him?'

'They'll get him,' said somebody.

'It all happened so quickly,' said someone else.

'How about going to the hospital for a check-up, fella?'

I was focusing things a lot better now. I grunted, doubled one leg beneath me, tried to clamber to my feet. They had to help me, guide me across to the bar-counter. I stood there, holding on to the counter, trying to get my sense of balance under control.

The cafe was crowded with folk, earnest, serious-faced folk. I caught a glimpse of uniforms, grey fedoras and hard-faced men with steel grey eyes. One of them was pushing his way through the crowd towards me. He stared at me with eyes that penetrated to my backbone.

'Feel like talking yet, Mac?' he asked.

I passed the back of my hand across my forehead. It came away glistening with water and tainted with diluted blood. My fingers crawled up towards the top of my scalp. It was tender, on fire. 'That guy sure slugged me, I croaked.

'That's the idea,' he said approvingly. 'Let's have a statement.'

I looked around hazily. Somebody anticipated me, pushed a glass into my hand. I lapped the brandy gratefully. I needed it.

'All you've got to do is state exactly what happened. No frills. Get the idea?'

'Yeah,' I said weakly. 'I get the idea.'

A tubby little guy wearing glasses pushed his way out from a group of dicks at the other end of the cafe.

I stared at him.

I felt the roof of my mouth go dry. I asked hoarsely: 'Ain't that Doc Gilson?'

The dick gave him a casual glance. 'Sure,' he said. 'Something strange about him?'

There was for me. Because Doc Gilson was a police doctor, and I was remembering I'd collected none of those six shots that had been fired. I pushed the dick roughly to one side, thrust my way through the crowd surrounding me, walked unsteadily to the far end of the cafe and shouldered through dicks and cops.

She didn't look any different now, except her eyes were closed. They'd straightened her out so she was lying quiet and peaceful, almost like she was sleeping. They'd placed her hands together on her breasts, and her uppermost hand wore the engagement ring.

There was only a little blood. A few flecks on her blouse and a tiny dried-up trickle from the corner of her mouth.

I said in a choked voice: 'Where did she get it? Where did it hit her?'

A cop said quietly: 'Smashed through her spine, musta glanced off and penetrated her lung. Couldn't have lived more than a few seconds afterwards.'

It was hard to believe. A few moments earlier, she had been sitting there happily contemplating her future.

Now she was lying still and lifeless, already stiffening in death.

'Who was she?' asked the dick over my shoulder.

'I don't know,' I said numbly.

'You were with her, weren't you?'

'Sure,' I said, and I was having difficulty in thinking.

'You've gotta start talking, fella,' he urged. 'You've gotta tell us everything. What do you know about her?'

I stared at her, eyes closed, face quiet and composed in eternal sleep.

'She was gonna be married next Monday,' I said tonelessly.

6

The guy had been right about one thing. He'd given me a red-hot story.

The cops let me phone the *Chicago Chronicle* before I went down to Headquarters. It took four hours of painful discussion and questioning to convince them I hadn't the faintest idea who the guy was, why he should want to shoot me or that I had no relationship with the dame.

Long before I got back to the office, the midday *Chronicle* was on the streets, with blazing headlines about just one more killing.

And if I'd felt bad before, now I felt ten times worse. I had a head that was splitting in two as well as being an intolerable weight. My eyes were set in gritty beds of sand that scratched and seared.

I pushed through the throng of reporters in the Newsroom who wanted to congratulate me on my narrow escape, sat down at my desk and rested my head in my hands. I wasn't good for anything except going home to bed, and I hadn't even got the strength to do that now.

A messenger sidled alongside my desk, slid a sheet of paper under my nose. I groaned inwardly, opened my pained eyes and stared down at a neatly-typed report.

Without enthusiasm and quite automatically I began to read. And the more I read, the more my tiredness evaporated. The Information Department had been working efficiently, and had prepared a very full report on Greigs.

And the more I read of that report, the more I thought of Cora. And the more I thought of Cora, the more I wanted to laugh, although after what I had been through I didn't think there was a laugh left inside me.

It was all there, information that Cora would have given her ears to learn. And things weren't one little the way Cora thought.

The old guy was practically penniless!

Practically penniless according to Cora's ideas, that is. In a nutshell, Cora was right off beam. Because the only moneybags in the Greigs family was Greigs' suicidal wife.

Information Department musta dug deep to find the information they had given me. Old man Greigs had led a blameless life, was a professor of sorts. He'd been to college, obtained degrees, taught students, and finally became accepted as a specialist in archaeology. He probably pulled down enough to live modestly.

The first time he married was at the age of thirty-five The marriage had lasted fifteen years, at the end of which time his wife died suddenly. He'd married his present wife just five years ago, and his age to date was sixty-five.

And Greigs hadn't a penny!

Much more interesting reading was the report on Greigs' wife. Rosa Greigs was an orphan. But a wealthy uncle and aunt had undertaken to take care of her. The uncle and aunt had been rich folk, good-living but cranky. They believed it their duty to take care of Rosa Greigs and her brother, yet at the same time were sociologists, had an overwhelming urge to make the world a better place to live in.

Their interest in crackpot societies was the only explanation for the oddness of their will.

Just recently, Rosa Greigs' uncle and aunt had been killed in a road accident. The terms of their will stated their house and the income from their investments go to Rosa Greigs for so long as she lived in the house and did not vacate it for more than one month in any one year. Should Rosa Greigs die, the house and the fitments were left in their entirety to a named charity for orphaned children. No provisions were made in the will for Mrs Greigs' brother, Tony Gilmore. Presumably aunt and uncle assumed Tony would be able to take care of himself.

Yeah, it was comical to think of Cora devoting her talents in that direction. Old Greigs could live in comfort as long as his wife lived. But if his wife died, Greigs would have to clear out quickly. Additionally, since it was a large house, the income from the dwindling investments was just about enough to enable them to live comfortably, and pay the expenses of the house. No chance of saving dough.

With that information, I sure could save Cora a whole lot of heartbreak.

But I didn't intend to!

It wasn't the end of the report. There was more to it. The uncle and aunt had added a clause to their will. After the death of Rosa Greigs, the administration of the estate was to handled by Warren Anderson, upon whom was placed the responsibility of handling the finances and transferring the property and the investments to the orphans' home. Mr Warren Anderson was a solicitor, and I'd met him at Greigs' house.

There was additional interesting information about Rosa Greigs herself. Twice in the past five years she'd tried to commit suicide. Twice she'd been before the courts for this offence, and medical advisers had pleaded temporary insanity. She was a quiet, retiring woman, shy of making friends and never wanting to go out.

Greigs had been her next-door neighbour for almost ten years before he had known her well enough to propose.

It was probably the only chance Rosa ever had to marry, and she accepted his proposal promptly. When Rosa's uncle and aunt were killed in a car crash, the Greigs found themselves in the big money, moved into their present, sumptuous, luxurious house.

Yeah, the laugh was on Cora. But it was on me too. Because thinking about Cora was something I shouldn't have started. It was like there was a cord attached from me to her little finger and I was dangling like a puppet. I tried to push all thoughts of her out of my mind, but I couldn't stop thinking about her. The memory of her kept mocking me, the pertness of her face, the deep wisdom of her eyes and the inviting creaminess of her bared breasts.

Three times I reached for the phone and then stopped myself. The fourth time I went all the way, picked up the phone, before I remembered I didn't know the number.

Moreover, the chances were she was already resident in Greigs' home, scheming her future with the skill and subtly of a spider spinning its web.

It would be easy to ring Greigs' home and ask for her. But the commonsense inside me was fighting the impulse. Or maybe it was pride and not commonsense. She'd have given my pride an awful beating, and I knew I'd have to take more if I wanted to see her, I'd have to humble myself, plead with her to meet me. My resolve slowly strengthened. If a dame doesn't meet you on even terms, you're licked. You're licked if you chase after a dame, because when a dame's got you dangling that way, there's only one smart thing to do. Cut all connections, keep well away from her and forget about her if you can.

Because when a dame's got the edge on you, it's slow poison. You chase after her, and the more persistent you become, the more contemptuous and disinterested she is. Your pride is humbled and you lose confidence in yourself.

I put her out of my mind.

She came back.

I put her out of my mind again, tried to forget her cheeky face, those wise eyes and her rich, creamy breasts.

She kept coming back.

I knew I was already half beat, knew that I was gonna have a tough time restraining myself from chasing after her. Knew that if I did, I would hear her mocking chuckle ringing in my ears and know the bitter disappointment of failure.

The telephone rang.

It startled me, I was sweating. I'd been fighting so hard to restrain my impulse to go out and find her that I'd worked up a lather.

I reached for the phone, and it was slippery in my hand. I pressed the receiver to my ear and said, hoarsely: 'Newsroom.'

She said, diffidently: 'Oh. Is that you?'

My heart leaped, and then started beating double tempo. Just hearing her on the phone again was a physical and nervous shock. 'Yeah ' I said hoarsely. 'This is me.'

'When can we meet?' she asked sweetly.

I could feel the blood hammering in my head, feel it pulsing thick and rich through my body. Those wise eyes were smiling at me, and white, creamy flesh was inviting and irresistible. But she was trouble, trouble all the way. Because to her, I didn't mean a thing.

I said slowly and with an effort: 'What have we got to meet about?'

The note of surprise in her voice was genuine. 'Don't you want to see me again?'

'Maybe,' I said cautiously.

'Okay. If you don't, that's all there is to it,' she said indifferently.

'Wait a minute,' I gasped quickly, afraid she was going to hang up. And then, reluctant to give her an advantage, I asked: 'Is it something special you want to see me about?'

'Nothing special,' she said coolly. 'I thought you might like to take me to dinner.' I could almost see her shrugging her shoulders. 'But it's not important.'

'Where shall I meet you?' I croaked.

'Wanna pick me up?'

'What time?'

'About eight,' she suggested. 'Remember the house?'

'I'll be there,' I said. 'Dead on the nail.'

I put down the phone with my brain in a whirl, thinking about her, intoxicated by the memory of her voice, sensing again the way she'd been pressed close against me, seeing those eyes, so compelling, so knowledgeable, so irresistible.

I was abruptly brought back to the world of reality by a cold, acid voice. 'Have you cornered the world market for sticking plaster, or is that the only way she could get away?'

I glanced up into grey eyes that were bitter and contemptuous, quailed beneath the quiet lash of her tongue. I worked up a weak grin. 'Hiya, Scallywag,' I said.

'The name's Lang,' she said sharply. 'Sheila Lang. And my associates are supposed to call me *Miss Lang.*'

'Come off it, kid,' I growled.

She shook her head, auburn hair rippling like captured sunbeams. 'It was one time too many, Hank. I'm through this time for sure. It gets so that every time I meet you, I'm tangled up in some other dame's underclothes, perfume or troubles. I can't take it anymore.'

'Listen, honey,' I said. 'I can explain everything. The other night, you misunderstood. What happened was ...'

She cut in crisply, overtaking me. 'This isn't a social cell, Hank. I'm here on business.'

'To hell with business. It's you that matters. You've got to understand ...'

She said, slowly and evenly: 'I don't want to hear explanations, Hank. It's all finished. Understand? I came here to ask you just one question. You can answer it or not, as you like. But we're all washed-up. Understand?'

I knew Sheila well. Sometimes I figured I knew her better than she knew herself. She was in one of those moods when it was impossible to reason with her. Maybe some other time when she'd softened.

I sighed. 'Okay, kid,' I said. 'What's on your mind?'

'A guy named Greigs.'

I stared at her.

She stared back, and there was sullen suspicion at the back of her eyes.

'What about Greigs?'

'You've asked Information Department to dig up dope on him.'

'Sure,' I said. 'Did I do something wrong?'

'What are you after, Hank? I know you by now. You've got

your nose into something. And if you've got any hunches about Greigs, I wanna know about them. It's important.'

I was getting out of my depth. I had the uneasy feeling Sheila had been checking up on me, might even have learned about Cora. I drew a deep breath, said softly: 'I'll make a trade. Tell me why you're interested in Greigs and I'll tell you why I'm interested.'

She said crisply, her voice flat and even: 'It's about that archaeological find they made down in Idaho. Remember? Gold prospectors found the ruins of an ancient town, unearthed ancient pottery and glassware.'

My eyes widened. 'Since when have you taken an interest in archaeology?'

'I edit the woman's page, remember?' she said sharply. 'Women aren't so dumb as you think. They're interested in all kinds of things. Right now, they're good and interested in those archaeological discoveries.'

'And how does Greigs fit in?'

'Because there's reason to believe some of these utensils are of Roman origin, and Greigs is a specialist on Roman history. He's had some of the relics sent to him to examine and report upon.'

'What do I have to do? Cry my eyes out?'

'Listen, bighead,' she snapped. 'Those relics are priceless. A thousand collectors would give their ears to get hold of them. If you've any reason to suspect there's anything crooked about Greigs, I ought to know before something happens to those relics.'

I chuckled.

I laughed.

I shook with laughter, dabbed my eyes with my handkerchief, couldn't even cease when her small, hard fist jagged my ribs viciously.

'What's so funny, you big ape?' she demanded irritably.

'You,' I chuckled. 'Rooting around for a big story when all that's involved is tittle-tattle for the woman's page.'

'It's your turn to talk,' she snarled. 'What makes you so

interested in Greigs?'

'You really wanna know?' I grinned.

Her eyes were hard and biting. 'It's a trade. Remember?'

'Okay,' I said, and there was a snap in my voice now. 'Greigs' wife fell in the river the other night. I fished her out. Remember? I told you about it and you wouldn't believe me. I put in a check on Greigs out idle curiosity.'

Her eyes were still hard. 'You're coming clean, Hank?' she persisted.

'Sure, honey,' I said. 'That's all there is to it.'

'There's nothing more behind it?'

'Nothing at all, honey,' I assured her.

Her eyes snapped fire. 'Then how come you got perfume all over your jacket after it'd been dried off?'

'That,' I said with dignity, 'is an explanation I shall give when I feel you merit it.'

She glared at me. 'Smartie, huh?'

'No, kid,' I said. 'Not smart. Just plain awkward.'

I watched her as she scornfully clip-clopped away from me on high heels, her flared skirt swaying from side to side, her head high, jaw jutting and every line of her body expressing hurt, indignation.

Seeing her walk that way, every inch of her throbbing nth outraged femininity and the movements of her body subtle and sinewy, made me think of that other one.

I didn't want to think about her, I didn't want to see her. I wanted to keep well away from her. But I had to see her. She had something that appealed to me. And the hell of it was, I didn't know what made her so different.

Whatever it was had got me.

I didn't wanna meet her. I knew it was gonna cause me grief seeing her again, and I was steeling myself, telling myself I was gonna ditch her, leave her waiting, leave her to figure out why I hadn't turned up and to learn I wasn't a puppet dangling on the end of a thread.

Then I glanced at my watch to make sure I had time to get home and change before I picked her up.

7

She must have seen me coming from her window, because she was at the front door as I pulled into the kerb.

It was a squalid neighbourhood. The neighbours stared frankly and curiously as she clip-clopped down the steps on inordinately high heels and climbed into the car beside me. She was wearing a thin skirt pinched tight with a patent black belt, and it rode up high, revealing the silken gleam of nylons as she pulled the car door shut after her.

'All set,' I growled. I was self-conscious at having a battery of eyes turned upon me.

She was enjoying the publicity. She shook out her hair, settled back comfortably against the upholstery, adjusted her short bolero jacket. 'Okay,' she breathed. 'Let's go.'

I let in the clutch, got the car rolling, and the eyes followed, raked us mercilessly. She was holding her head high, smiling slightly, proud at the attention she was receiving.

I raced through the gears, got clear of that district as quickly as I could. She didn't say anything, and I wasn't in a talking mood.

But I was acutely conscious she was sitting there beside me!

She'd swamped herself in her cheap perfume. It washed over me gently, breathtaking and reminiscent, conjuring up intimate memories, the smell of her skin, the softness of her cheek, the hard urgency inside her as she strained against me.

I threaded my way across town, headed out through the

suburbs on to the Eastern Road. 'Where we going?' she asked disinterestedly.

'A little place I know. I think you'll like it.'

'Roadhouse, huh?'

I shot her a frigid glance. 'Anywhere else you suggest is okay by me.'

'Suits me fine,' she said, and crossed her legs. She was deliberately careless about it. The fine sheen of nylon showed from well above her knee. And the skirt was so thin, it clung to her thighs like another skin. If she was wearing anything at all beneath that skirt, it had to be very little, because it didn't show.

'Have you got a cigarette?'

'Sure,' I said. 'In my pocket. Help yourself.'

She moved over close against me, much closer than was necessary. She delved into my pocket with a skilful movement that caused her hair to brush against my cheek, pressed her knee hard against my thigh, allowed me to feel the weight of her breast resting on my forearm.

'Cut it out,' I growled. 'We've been all through that. It doesn't get us anywhere.'

She chuckled, moved away from me ever so slightly so that I could still feel the contact of her. 'You're cute,' she whispered.

'Sure. I'm the cat's whiskers. Now quit driving me crazy, will you?'

'You want a cigarette?'

Her face was close to mine, eyes smiling at me. I wouldn't look at her. 'Yeah,' I grunted. 'I might as well smoke if I'm liable to go up in flames any minute.'

She lit two cigarettes at the same time, pressed against me as she placed the cigarette between my lips, so that I was almost suffocated by the smell of her scent and driven half-crazy by the soft touch of her hair and the warm, lithe insinuating movements of her body.

The end of the cigarette was damp, flaked with greasy lipstick. But to me it tasted as sweet and as fragrant as water from the spring of eternal life.

'You're being stuffy,' she sulked, and her knee was pressing against my thigh meaningfully, all of her a calculated tantalisation.

'What are you trying to prove?' I growled. 'You've shown you can do it. You can make me turn somersaults. Why the repeat performance? We've got no audience.'

Her fingers stole around my shoulder, and her cheek rested against my shoulder. 'Don't you like me, honey?' she whispered coyly, and her breath was hot, moist and intimate.

'A real glutton for flattery,' I accused.

'Not altogether,' she said seriously, and I could feel her eyes groping for mine, trying to obtain control over me.

'Be smart, sister,' I growled. 'You can pull that trick once, but you can't do it a second time. Lay off me, will ya? You're not getting yourself anywhere and you're not getting me anyway, either.'

She wasn't offended, she chuckled, stretched herself like a cat, said smoothly: 'Okay, honey. If that's the way you want it.'

She moved away from me gently without appearing to do so, coiled her legs beneath her so she could sit sideways with her arm along the back of the seat, staring at me, amusement glinting in her eyes.

I kept on driving. I wouldn't look at her.

'A real tough type,' she commented mockingly. 'Tough, relentless and unemotional.'

'That's me,' I grunted. 'I'm immune. It's like being vaccinated. One tiny shot of what's bad for you makes you immune when the disease catches up with you later on.'

'And now you don't have to worry about me one little bit,' she said mockingly.

I gritted my teeth. 'That's just the way it is.'

'How nice for you, and how comfortable for me,' she teased, and uncrossed her legs, pulled down her skirt.

She'd given in too easily. She wasn't the type of dame who admits her charms have no avail. She knew, and I suspected, she'd only just completed the first move towards my complete subjugation.

'Now tell me about the weather,' she said, and smiled

wickedly.

I half-growled, half-snarled: 'I shouldn't have met you. It was crazy. This ain't gonna earn me anything but grief.'

I could feel her cool eyes resting upon me. It needed an effort not to look at her. 'But you came,' she insisted. 'You came, didn't you?'

'Once in a while, a guy does something he knows shouldn't'

Her voice was still mocking. 'Are you all that much afraid of me?'

I took a deep breath. 'Sure,' I said. 'I'm scared stiff.' And the strange thing was, I almost meant it.

I said: 'We turn off the main road here.'

She watched disinterestedly as I made a full right-angle turn and got onto a second-class road that twisted and turned through the countryside like an enormous snake. The sun was setting now, casting a golden sheen over green foliage, reflecting on her face so that she seemed to be glowing with an inner warmth.

'Will I have to walk home this trip?' she asked, and a smile was rippling through her words. Then with startling abruptness, I was seeing again the creamy swell of her bared breasts as she'd displayed her torn blouse, and felt inside me the desire to nestle my head close against her, feel her feminine warmth and softness.

'The chances are, it will be me doing the walking,' I growled.

That amused her. She really did laugh then. Not a mocking laugh, but a ripple of pure merriment. 'I *have* got you worried, haven't I?' she mocked.

I ignored that comment, made a sharp right turn along a tree-lined driveway towards the roadhouse.

It wasn't a showy joint and it wasn't a swanky joint. It was a place to get a good meal in pleasant surroundings without tinsel, pompousness or stiff shirt fronts.

The garden was a maze of hedges and trees, slung with Chinese lanterns and fairy lamps.

A shirt-sleeved waiter showed us to a table nestled away out of sight from the other diners, discreetly surrounded by trimmed hedges. From the branches of an overhanging tree, lanterns dangled, throwing a warm glow over us. The table lamp threw a carefully-shaded light on the red-and-white-checked table cloth. The table was made from rough-hewn trees, embedded in the ground. The chairs were rustic style, upholstered with folk-weave cushions.

She smiled approvingly. 'It's kinda cute here.'

The shirt-sleeved waiter beamed happily. 'The food's good too, lady,' he said.

'What's special tonight?' I asked.

'Anything you want, we've got. Any way you want it cooked, we cook it.'

'Service, huh?'

'That's the way we keep our customers.'

It was a warm evening, so we started with ham salad, settled for chilli-con-carne for the second dish, and had a bottle of red burgundy to wash it down.

We were facing each other across the table, and she wasn't fooling me any. She was playing with me, playing with me the way a cat plays with a mouse.

The hell of it was, I didn't even want to escape.

Halfway through the meal, I felt her dainty shoe press against my foot. I didn't move. A few moments later, she moved her other foot, imprisoned my foot between hers.

I started sweating.

Her amused eyes were mocking and calculating.

'D'you like the food?' I asked hoarsely.

'Best I've tasted in weeks.'

I tried not to meet her eyes, was acutely conscious of the way she was imprisoning my foot beneath the table. I dabbed my mouth with the napkin, reached hurriedly for the wine. I poured clumsily, spilt some on the tablecloth, and all the time those cool, calculating eyes were watching, mocking and amused.

'I've got a theory,' I told her.

She leaned forward across the table, all attentive, eyes half-closed, waiting and expectant.

'I probably ain't the first guy to hold this theory,' I admitted.

'Do tell,' she coaxed.

'I figure dames are hell!'

'Am I hell, darling?'

'Quit riding me,' I pleaded. 'Why don't you leave me in peace? You know you don't want anything with all this. I'm not the guy you want. I haven't got any dough.'

She said softly: 'Don't you want me to be nice to you, honey?'

'Sure I do. But I don't like a train leaving me halfway to my destination.'

'Maybe you didn't sit tight long enough.'

'Could be,' I admitted. 'But it didn't look that way to me.'

She said softly, coaxingly: 'I could be nice to you, honey, if you were nice to me.'

A cold finger of suspicion touched my brain. I could feel myself tensing all over. 'Just how could I be nice to you?'

'Get us an invitation to visit the Greigs',' she said bluntly.

I'd been deliberately holding back. Now she'd brought up the subject, I waded in. 'What happened?' I demanded. 'Aren't you supposed to be working for him today? Weren't you getting your claws sharpened up ready to gouge them deep in his shoulders?'

She was calm and unruffled, her eyes smiling. 'It didn't work out, honey. He sent a messenger. Said he didn't really need help at his house but recommended me for a job in the house of a neighbour.'

'Gave you the cold shoulder, huh?'

Her eyes flashed angrily for a second. 'After saving his wife's life, too!'

'Yeah,' I echoed drily. 'After you saved his wife's life!'

She had to smile at that. 'Anyway he does owe me something.'

'He knows that,' I said. 'He's offered to recommend you for a job with a neighbour.'

'D'you want me to be nice to you?' she asked bluntly.

I sat back in my chair, took a deep breath. 'It depends on just how nice you can be.'

She leaned across the table, her eyes narrowed, her voice tense. 'Greigs owes you something,' she said tersely. 'Get him on the phone, wangle an invitation to dinner. Take me along with you. I've got to get to know him better. He can't refuse you an invitation.'

I sat in my chair as cold as stone, the impulse strong inside me to throw my napkin straight in her face, climb to my feet and stalk away leaving her cold.

But I didn't do it. Because I was remembering the other side of the picture, remembering something she didn't know. Remembering that Greigs was penniless.

And suddenly the set-up was wonderful. Here she was, offering to be specially nice if I'd take her to dinner with Greigs. The irony of it was that it wouldn't do her the slightest good.

I relaxed slowly, trying to keep my voice controlled and my face emotionless. I said quietly. 'I wish you'd lay off Greigs.'

'Is it a deal?' she asked quietly.

'You've got the wrong angle, kid,' I said. 'You can't live this way.'

Her eyes snapped. 'You leave me to decide that.'

I shrugged my shoulders. 'Okay,' I said. 'It's a deal, I'll wangle us an invitation for dinner with Greigs. But no strings.'

She arched one eyebrow. 'No strings?' Her voice was curious.

'It's for free.' I said with satisfaction. 'I'll wangle the invitation, and I'm not asking anything in return.'

She kinda flushed, and an unusual softness came into her eyes. 'You're being really sweet to me, honey,' she said, and her quiet acceptance of my offer caused my heart to drop. Because having her being nice to me was something that right then meant more than anything else to me.

'How about his wife?' she asked. 'Have you heard how she is?'

'So far as I know, you're unlucky. She hasn't died yet,' I said brutally.

Her eyes were mocking and laughing. 'Don't worry. I won't

let the grass grow under my feet.'

I eyed her cautiously. With a dame like her, so purposeful, it could just be possible she could really intend murder and be flippant about it at the same time.

'You wouldn't really try anything?' I asked doubtfully.

'Not by myself,' she smiled. 'I'd need help. Greigs himself maybe will give me a hand.'

She was joking. The tone of her voice and the words she used showed that. But even so, it could happen just the way she was suggesting.

I leaned forward across the table, looked straight into her eyes. Both my fists were clenched tightly. I said, slowly and deliberately: 'She's a young woman. If anything should happen to her, anything that wasn't an accident, nobody would get away with it. I wouldn't like it, the cops wouldn't like it, and Mrs Greigs' relatives wouldn't like it. None of us would rest until ...' I tailed off, leaving her to imagine the rest of the sentence.

Maybe she took me seriously, maybe not. It was hard to tell. She said, airily: 'Don't worry, honey. If I bump her off, it'll be the perfect murder. Nobody would able to pin anything on me.'

I sat looking at her across the table, and I didn't know whether to be amused or scared stiff.

The waiter coughed discreetly, scuffed his feet loudly as he approached to ask if we needed anything else.

We'd finished coffee by this time, I asked for the bill.

And I was worried now; I wasn't sure about her. Couldn't figure out if a dangerous undercurrent flowed beneath the surface smoothness of her joking.

She took my arm as we made our way to the car. Her fingers gripped tightly and intimately. When I climbed into the driving seat, she pushed up close against me, locked her arm in mine, rested her head on my shoulder.

It was what I wanted. I wanted her as close as that and much closer. But I only wanted her that way if she really wanted me. I didn't want favours for services rendered.

I steeled myself to conceal my reactions, drove to town like a robot seated at the wheel and driving with mechanical precision.

My attitude didn't worry her any. She snuggled even closer against me, half-drowsily, humming the latest swing number as we drove along.

There were no street lamps in front of the tenement block in which she lived. I was thankful for that, pulled into the kerb, switched off the engine and carefully edged her away from me.

She sat up straight with an easy grace, fluffed up her hair, climbed out of the car, looked at me expectantly.

'I'll be seeing you,' I growled.

Her eyes were wide and surprised. 'But it's early. Aren't you coming up?'

Every fibre of my being was straining towards her. But my brain was shouting No. NO!

And my tongue was a traitor. My tongue said: 'Yeah. Why not?'

The stairs were dimly lighted. Her hand brushed mine on the banister rail, and she hesitated on one step so that, following close behind her, my chest bumped her rear. She chuckled over her shoulder. 'Don't get lost, honey.'

She opened up the door of her room with a latchkey, switched on the light, and I followed inside.

It was even more untidy than when I'd first visited her, the bedclothes rumpled, underclothing draped across chairs, or thrown carelessly in a corner, and the remains of a meal on the table. The room needed a good sweep, followed by a scrub with hot water and disinfectant.

She swept a handful of dirty underclothing from a chair and stuffed it away in a bulging chest-of-drawers.

'Make yourself at home,' she invited, as she stripped off her bolero.

I sat uncomfortably on the edge of the chair, watched as she strained up on tip-toe to hang her bolero on a hook behind the door.

Straining herself taut that way, and wearing that thin skirt, outlined the curves of her body clearly. It still looked to me like she was wearing nothing beneath that skirt. And the blouse she was wearing, Hungarian style with blue ribbons at the neckline and the upper arms, bore an intricate perforated design through which I could see the soft gleam of her skin. It didn't reveal any brassiere straps.

She turned around quickly, like she knew I was eyeing her and wanted to catch me at it.

She caught me!

Her eyes were amused and mocking. She came towards me, walking carefully, deliberately swaying her body and hips rhythmically. At the same time, she pulled down the hem of her blouse, tucked it inside the black patent leather belt in a way that caused the fine material to form folds that led straight as arrows to the sharp-pointed extremities of her jutting breasts.

She used a low, husky tone when she asked: 'What do you want to drink?'

I gulped, concentrated on staring at that black leather belt. It was the safest place to look. 'Anything you've got,' I said hoarsely.

'Rye?'

Her eyes were watching me shrewdly, mockingly. I wouldn't look up at her. 'Sure,' I muttered. 'That'll do.'

She crossed to the chest-of-drawers, opened up the lowest drawer, dug down in it and came up with a bottle of rye and two glasses.

She inspected the glasses critically, reached for a stocking dangling over a chair back, used that to wipe the glasses clean.

'That ain't the way to treat stockings,' I said sarcastically.

My sarcasm ran off her like water off a duck's back. 'It's okay,' she said casually. 'They've got to be washed anyway.'

She poured a good four fingers of rye into each glass, brought my glass over to me, stood staring down at me mockingly as she handed me the glass. I could see the curve of her thighs through that thin material, could almost feel the heat of them flaming out at me. I reached for the glass with a shaking hand, and still avoided looking into her face.

'Down the hatch,' she said.

I sipped, and to my surprise it was good rye. She swallowed a third of hers in one gulp, sauntered slowly to the bed, swaying her hips, making sure that I could see how vibrant and supple were her limbs.

She switched on the table lamp beside the bed before she half-sat, half-reclined on the bed, and this time her eyes caught mine, held them.

It was like we were looking at each other for an eternity.

She said softly, subtly: 'Give me a cigarette.'

I didn't want to. I knew I was crazy. I knew that when you feel this way about a dame, it's better to run and keep running. But I couldn't save myself. I dug down in my pocket, came up with a pack.

'Don't throw it,' she said softly. 'Bring it.'

I got up slowly, went over to her carrying my drink. She lay back when I reached her, looked up at me with half-narrowed eyes and opened her lips so I could give her the cigarette. And all the time she was watching me.

My hands were trembling as I struck a match. And at the same time, she pressed the wall switch that turned off the main light. It left us united but alone in the soft glow of the bedside lamp.

'Can't you keep your hand still?' she asked mockingly as I held the match.

I was gripping my glass so tightly I was scared it would break. She leaned her head forward to place the end of the cigarette in the flame, sucked it into life, gave me one encouraging, sweeping glance from those eyes, and then lay right back on the pillow, raising her hands languorously to cradle her head, deliberately flaunting herself.

I raised my glass slowly to my lips, watching her all the time. Her body was a hot flame licking up towards me, an irresistible allure that could engulf me entirely, consume me in one great, white-hot conflagration.

I tilted my head, gulped the contents of my glass, felt the raw spirit burn my throat and tongue, felt the smart of it at the back of my eyes, making them watery. Then slowly and deliberately I placed my glass down on the table beside her.

Her half-closed eyes were still watching me, inviting but at the same time smiling mockingly. I reached out, plucked the cigarette from between her lips, ground it on the floor beneath my heel.

The half-closed eyes smiled even more mockingly. That was the only emotion she showed.

I said, softly: 'Damn you.'

She moved her body, lazily, sensuously.

I slammed the butt of my hand down on the light switch of the table lamp and, as darkness engulfed us, I went down at her.

Her mouth was ripe, moist and soft. The smell of her and the smell of her perfume was clogging my nostrils as her lips responded. Then suddenly she wasn't mocking and contemptuous. Her hands were around me, beneath my jacket, nails digging into my shoulders, her mouth and body moving in a kinda blind, unleashed surge of emotion. Her mouth was everything, alive and vital, lips rich and hot, drawing me close to her, consuming me. And suddenly I was crazy too, wanting to crush her, drawing her close to me to be a part of me, wanting to feel her strength diminish until I had drawn it all from her.

She wrenched her head away, twisted her lips from mine, and the rigidity of her fingers and the warring nails gouging into my shoulders were an unspoken command to lie still.

In the darkness, her breathing was strangely loud. The pulsing of her heart was hammering through me and the taste of her lips was still hot and sweet on mine.

And rigid fingers and gouging nails were yet a command to keep still. Quite still!

Slowly her breathing eased.

She whispered the words and I couldn't hear them.

'What's that?' I asked. 'What d'ya say?'

'Damn you,' she panted, not very much louder. 'You've almost got me on the hop.'

'I'm not exactly ice-cold myself.'

'That you don't need to tell me!'

I hooked my hand around the back of her neck, gathered up her hair, levered on it to drag her face around to mine and crush her lips hard against mine. She fought me all the time, twisting her head away, her lips responsive but trying not to be.

I let her go again, and her breath was harsh and rasping.

'So this is the end of the line?' I said bitterly.

She didn't answer, just lay there breathing heavily. But when I tried to slip away, her arms held me tightly, the tips of her nails digging into my shoulders with a sweet sharpness.

We lay that way for almost five minutes until the hot pulsing of her body had calmed and her breathing was soft and even.

'What happens now?' I demanded.

Gently she pushed me away from her, levered herself around so we were sitting side by side on the edge of the bed. She said, with a faint note of surprise in her voice: 'I wasn't reckoning on this.'

'Sure you weren't,' I snarled sarcastically. 'You figured we'd play dominoes.'

She said: 'Don't move,' and one hand rested restrainingly on my shoulder as she climbed to her feet.

I could see the dim outline of her in the darkness as she stood the other side of the bed doing something I couldn't see. I heard the tiny sound of her nails against leather.

'What goes on?' I demanded.

'Wait a minute,' she whispered hoarsely.

There was a soft but vaguely familiar sound.

'What are you doing?' I asked again.

'My skirt,' she whispered. 'I don't want to get it creased.' As she spoke, I heard the soft whisper of it against her thighs as it fell to the ground.

Emotion overcame me suddenly. A hot wave so powerful it made me momentarily faint. I relaxed back on the pillows, closed my eyes.

The springs creaked slightly as her weight came down on them. I could sense her there, stretching out her body luxuriously with a kinda animal pride in its luxurious sensitivity.

Through the darkness, her hand found the back of my neck, pulled my lips towards hers, the soft, pliant warmth of her enveloping, compelling and powerful.

My face was buried in the softness of her hair, and my senses were swimming with her drowsy, breathtaking perfume. Her skin was hot and burning, lips greedy and lascivious, like there wasn't gonna be anything hold her back now she'd let herself go.

But I still wasn't sure. She'd made a fool of me once before. It would be unbearable if I let myself respond, only to find that for the second time she was playing with me.

It needed an effort to pull my lips away from hers. I said hoarsely. 'It's no go. I can't pay the price you want.'

She didn't answer. There was only the sound of her heavy breathing as she searched for my lips.

I jerked my head back, averted my face. I was sweating all over, trembling while her soft fingers stealing inside my shirt were a tingling magnetism.

'Better break it up,' I said hoarsely. I'm not falling for it a second time.'

Her body strained against me. She was suddenly possessed of an incredible strength, and through the darkness her breathing was jerky and spasmodic, like she'd been running uphill.

I had to break it up. I had to break it up now, because if I didn't, later would be too late. I pulled away from her.

She clung tenaciously.

'Let me go,' I said fiercely.

'No,' she panted.

Again I tried to pull away.

She kinda wrapped herself around me, added the weight of her body to the strength of her limbs.

'You're taking this too far,' I panted. 'You're taking too big a risk.'

She said faintly: 'It's what you want, isn't it?'

'Sure,' I said, and the sweat was running down from my

forehead, making my eyes smart.

She panted: 'You promised. You'll take me to dinner with Greigs?'

An ice-cold wave swept over me. Momentarily I was possessed by a blind, raging anger. I gripped her so tightly she squealed with the pain of it, and the sound sobered me, made me rigid with the sweat on my brow cold like drops of ice.

'You promised,' she said again, and her voice, arms and body were urging me.

I licked my lips. 'Yeah, that's right,' I growled, and my voice was throbbing with frustration. 'I promised.'

'I want you,' she whispered. 'I want you so much.'

There wasn't any doubting that. Her body arched up towards me, her nails sharp and goading.

But my reaction had an effect. The sweat was still ice-cold on my forehead. I pushed myself away from her rapidly, savagely and determinedly.

She grabbed at my hands, wrestled with me. 'No,' she panted. 'I want you. I want you.'

I gritted my teeth, put the back of my palm beneath her chin, thrust her backwards and got to my feet.

She was lying there in the darkness, panting heavily, eyen staring up at me.

'I'll fix that dinner appointment for you,' I gritted.

She said in a small, taut voice. 'Don't go. Don't you understand? Don't you understand what I want?'

'Sure,' I said bitterly. 'I know what you want. You want a husband with dough.'

Her voice was soft, tender and yearning, so that I almost broke down. 'This is different. I've never felt this way about anyone before.'

'Sure,' I said bitterly. 'This is different. You've played with fire once too often, set yourself alight.'

'Don't go,' she said suddenly, urgently.

But I was already across the room at the door. I heard the bed springs creak as I jerked at the door handle, heard her bare feet on the linoleum as I slipped through the door, closed it behind me.

She musta known instinctively she'd lost this round. She didn't try to follow me.

It was late. I clumped loudly down the stairs, my footsteps echoing resoundingly.

I was still sweating. I'd taken just about as much as any guy can take, and my underclothes were damp, sticking to me. I walked across to my car, unlocked the door, stood there mopping my forehead with clammy hands.

Yet a tiny corner of my brain was vaguely conscious of the lights of a car further along the street.

Subconsciously I heard the whir of the starter and the gentle throb of a powerful engine. I opened the door of my car as the other driver glided smoothly towards me.

That dame sure had put me in a lather. If she hadn't, maybe I'd have been more alert. As it was, it came as a complete surprise.

I ducked my head to climb into my car just as the other car came level. The roar of the gun and the impact of lead were simultaneous.

It was the edge of the door that saved me. Lead smashed into metal, twisting it out of shape, splintering glass and tearing the door from my grip so it smashed back against my head, stunning me. I half-fell, half-sprawled into the driving seat.

But even though I was half-dazed, my instinct of self-preservation was working. Automatically I drew my legs up, lunged for the glove box where I kept my Luger.

For sure the guy had seen me fall. Maybe he figured I'd got it. Because he kept right on driving, rammed his foot down on the accelerator and sped off into the night.

He'd been over-confident. If he'd dragged the car to a halt and pumped more shots at me, I shouldn't have had a chance. I still hadn't got my Luger out of the glove box when the soft purr of his engine had died away.

I stood up slowly, discovered I was trembling. This was the second time an unknown guy had taken a shot at me. And this time he'd nearly made it.

Nearly made it!

It had been a matter of an inch. An inch higher, and the bullet would have missed the car door, bored a hole right through my head. An inch lower, and it would have drilled a hole through glass before penetrating my skull.

I was shaking so badly I had to lean against the car for a few moments, light myself a cigarette.

It was the suddenness, the abrupt unexpectedness of it, that made it so shocking. I'd been thinking of Cora, the vitality of her youthful young body.

And then suddenly this. Lead spitting at me out of the night, almost blasting me into nothingness, missing me by a split second of time and position.

It was a quiet street. Then suddenly it wasn't so quiet. There came the rasp of windows being lifted, muffled voices, and the distant, all too familiar sound of the police siren.

I realised I was wasting time, that I was crazy sitting around trying to recover from a bad case of nerves. If I wanted to avoid hours at Police Headquarters trying to convince them I didn't take a shot at myself, the smart thing was to scram.

Quickly but unsteadily, I climbed in behind the driving wheel, started the engine, threw in the gear and drew away from the kerb.

There were at least half-a-dozen faces spying on me from curtained windows. But that didn't worry me any. I didn't think anyone was gonna tell the cops anything. I didn't think anyone was even gonna admit having heard or seen anything.

It was that kinda district.

8

I saw her entering the door at the far end of the office and deliberately buried my nose in a mass of proofs.

I heard her high heels clipping over to me, knew she was beside me, looking down at me.

Deliberately I didn't raise my eyes.

'All right, you big ape,' she growled. 'Don't try playing possum.'

'What d'you want, kid?' I said, without looking up. 'I'm busy. So don't take too long.'

'Cut it out, Hank,' she said. 'I know you like a book. It's no use. I'm not going to get hurt and worried because you pretend not to care if I'm here or not.'

Slowly I put down my pencil, pushed the proofs to one side, hooked my feet around my chair legs and rocked back precariously on the two rear legs.

'Okay, Scallywag,' I grinned. 'What's on your mind?'

'I want you to do a favour.'

'So that's it, huh? As soon as you want some help, you come running to me.'

She flushed, narrowed one eye dangerously. 'We're working on the same paper, remember? We're supposed to have a common aim. Or maybe you don't feel the way you used to.'

I flushed. 'What's on your mind? What can I do?'

'This guy Greigs,' she said slowly. 'You say you prevented his wife committing suicide. Is that on the level?'

I sighed. 'How many more times do I have to tell you?'

'How well d'you know Greigs?' she countered.

'Just that one time.'

'You know him enough to wangle an invitation to dinner?'

My chair legs came down with a bang. 'An invitation to dinner!' I echoed.

'What's the matter? Don't you hear so good these days?'

I looked her over slowly. She glared back at me.

'I'd never have believed it,' I said.

'Believed what?' she snapped.

I sighed. 'A guy's wife tries to commit suicide. And on account the guy's got dough and that his wife will maybe succeed next time she tries to kill herself, someone wants to meet him.'

Her lips were set in a hard, grim line. 'What kinda crack is that?'

'Not a crack. A blind guess.'

'Too much sun,' she diagnosed promptly. She added thoughtfully: 'Or maybe too many women.'

I tactfully changed the subject. 'Do I understand you want me to get an invitation from Greigs, so I can take you to dinner at his house?'

'You're smart,' she drawled, with mock awe. 'You catch on. You're going to go places, sonny.'

'Maybe I'm not so smart,' I said. 'I don't get it. Will you tell me exactly why I should take you to meet Greigs?'

'The reason is quite obvious, I should have thought,' she said tartly.

I stared at her incredulously. 'Don't tell me you've started gold digging.'

'You stupid ape,' she snapped irritably. 'I don't know Greigs. I don't even wanna know him. But he's the authority on these ancient Roman discoveries, and he won't talk to the press. I figured maybe if you introduced me to him it would be different.'

I nodded wisely. 'I get it now. I take you along to see the old guy. Over dinner, we start talking casually about Roman history, until he shows us the specimens. Then we keep him talking until finally you've got your article.'

'Go up to standard four next year,' she said acidly.

'And you want I should arrange everything?'

'Didn't I make myself clear?'

I sighed. 'Is tonight all right?'

'Tonight will be fine.'

'Any special dish you'd like him to cook for you?'

She shot me a withering glance. 'Can you fix it? That's all I wanna know.'

'Sure I can fix it,' I said. 'I've already fixed it. I'm gonna have dinner at Greigs' house tonight.'

'That's fine. All you've got to do is ask if you can bring a friend.'

'I'm already taking a friend.'

There was a silence, a long silence. Her under-lip quivered. She said, in a small voice: 'Another dame I suppose.'

It hurt me to say it, because it hurt her. 'Sure,' I said. 'It's another dame.'

'Well, maybe we'd better forget …'

'Don't worry,' I drawled. 'She's got an angle of her own. I can easily fix another invitation for you. But don't get any wrong ideas, Scallywag. I don't want you and Cora fighting, clawing yourselves and me at the same time.'

She bit her lip. 'Where'd you get these ideas. As though I'd fight over you!'

I sighed wearily. 'I'm just warning you. Come along if you want, but keep your claws sheathed. If you can't keep that nasty little temper of yours under control, don't come.'

Her green eyes flashed, glinted with anger, and her small, compact body vibrated with suppressed annoyance. 'Who said I can't keep my temper under control,' she demanded fiercely.

'Of course you can, honey,' I said soothingly. 'But sometimes you don't want to. Let this be one of the nights that you can. Huh?'

She said, icily: 'I wouldn't come at all if it wasn't for the *Chronicle*. My readers need that story.'

'You want that I should drop by and pick you up?'

'You sure it won't be too much trouble?' she asked sarcastically.

'About eight,' I told her. 'And be ready. Dames who aren't ready on time give me a pain.'

'I'll be ready,' she said fiercely. 'Just don't keep *me* waiting, that's all.'

I couldn't be late after that. I timed everything carefully, jabbed the doorbell of her flat with my thumb just as eight o'clock began to strike.

She opened up like she'd been sitting inside waiting for the bell to ring. And she didn't intend keeping me waiting. She was ready.

And she looked a real dish!

Her emerald green corduroy suit was a perfect setting for her gleaming red hair and her green eyes. She wore a crisp, white, wisp of a hat that trailed a spider-web veil tantalisingly across the upper part of her face. Her jacket was open to reveal a white silk blouse with a square neckline. And that neckline was just right, cut low enough to reveal the initial swell of her breasts but not so low it was too daring.

Practically any clothes looked good on Sheila. And where her figure was concerned, she was a pocket Venus, beautifully proportioned, perfectly made.

Tonight she looked a real dish.

I couldn't help it. 'Gee, you look swell, Scallywag,' I said, with genuine admiration.

Her eyes glistened and she seemed to radiate. 'Stop teasing, Hank,' she said brusquely. But I could tell she was as pleased as punch.

We took the lift down to the ground floor and I followed her across the entrance foyer, out through the awing doors and over to my car. On account she was small, she wore high-heeled shoes. She walked with a kinda high-stepping movement that made her hips roll and accentuated her curves. I could have followed her for miles.

I wasn't the only one who felt that way. At least half-a-dozen guys on the sidewalk turned their heads for a double-take, and one actually loitered, eyeing her shamelessly.

When I climbed in the driving seat alongside her, there was a pleased flush on her cheeks and a moist sparkle in her eyes. The silken sheen of her stockings showed off the smooth, symmetrical curves of her legs to perfection

'I've got to pick up this other dame,' I explained as I drew away from the kerb.

I heard her teeth click, and the flush on her cheeks became angry, and the sparkle in her eyes turned to a hard glint

'You don't know her,' I said faintly. 'It's probable you won't even like her. But you two have just gotta row along, for this evening at any rate.'

Sheila said, tersely: 'I hadn't figured on it being a joy-ride. I'm out on business.'

'Okay, so long as that's the way you behave.'

After that, there was an awkward kinda silence that continued until I drew up outside the tenement house where Cora lived.

Sheila glanced at it with undisguised disgust, shot me a scornful glance.

I bit my lip, applied the hand-brake, turned off the engine and climbed out from behind the wheel.

I was halfway up the steps when:

'Hey,' said Sheila.

I turned, eyed her enquiringly.

'What about me?'

'You wait.'

'I'd better come up.'

'It's not necessary,' I said.

Her eyes narrowed ominously. 'Listen, you big ape,' she rasped. 'If you think I'm gonna sit here being ogled by the neighbours, while you play hands with that dame upstairs, you've made a big mistake.'

I went back down the steps, opened up the car door. 'Okay,' I gritted. 'Come up if you want.'

She climbed the wooden, dimly-lighted stairs slowly and

disdainfully, careful not to touch either the walls or the banister.

When we reached Cora's room, I knocked on the door. There was a soft movement, and then, like she was shouting from the other side of the room: 'Is that you, Hank?'

'Yeah, it's me.'

'Come in. The door's not locked.'

Sheila was quicker off the mark than me, got her fingers wrapped around the door knob, pushed her way through inside. I hadn't figured on her doing that. But then, I hadn't figured on Cora being so far behind in getting ready.

It was difficult to say who was the more surprised, Cora or me. The only one who didn't seem surprised was Sheila. She let loose a disgusted *I-thought-so* kinda grunt, said tersely: 'Better close the door, Hank.'

But Cora was the first one to move. She'd been at the other side of the room with one bare foot resting on a chair as she bent over artistically to apply blood red nail polish to her toenails.

It was an artistic pose, probably carefully rehearsed, designed to give anyone who entered the door a perfect profile view of her figure. And it was a figure worthwhile profiling. Her thighs were perfectly rounded, her hips full and rich, her breasts hard and taut like soft fruit not quite ripe enough to be plucked. And so that anyone who came in that door shouldn't have difficulty in appreciating the youthful freshness of her body, Cora had failed to adorn her beauty. Almost failed, that is. Because, except for the flimsiest of white briefs, Cora was as naked as the day she was born.

And it was Cora who moved first.

She stared at Sheila with shocked eyes for a split second, squealed, lunged frantically for an article of underclothing, draped it strategically in front of her.

Sheila made a most unladylike noise. Half a grunt and half a snort of disgust.

Cora was breathing hard now, sullen and humiliated beneath the cold, scornful gaze of Sheila. I said, hoarsely: 'I thought you'd be ready, Cora. I've got a friend with me and ...'

'You shouldn't have burst in like that,' snapped Cora

angrily. Her eyes were glancing from me to Sheila with a kinda cold calculation.

Sheila said, with mocking sugary sincerity: 'Sorry to break in on you this way, honey. I'm sure Hank had no idea he'd catch you unawares.'

That was all!

But I knew right away war had been declared. I could sense both of them bristling, mentally groping for their battle weapons.

'Who the hell is she, anyway?' demanded Cora, and the fur she had drawn back from her nails, leaving them bared, ready to slash and rend.

'A friend of mine,' I said quickly, soothingly. 'Sheila, meet Cora. Mr Greigs has invited all three of us to dinner tonight.'

Sheila's fighting style was smoother, more skilful, and prettier to watch than that of Cora. She said: 'Of course, honey, we had no idea you wouldn't be ready. You must feel terribly embarrassed having us burst in on you this way.'

Sheila had made a preliminary trial slash to try out her opponent, and Cora didn't know how to counter. She made a feeble defence. 'I certainly didn't expect you,' she said pointedly.

'Never mind, honey,' smiled Sheila sweetly. 'Don't mind me. Continue doing all the things you want to do, just like I'm not here.'

Cora glared at her, numbly, lost for an answer.

I ran my finger round the neckband of my shirt, rasped in a hoarse, strained voice. 'Listen, you two. We're gonna be late. Snap it up, will ya? We can't keep Greigs waiting.'

'Yes, do hurry, honey,' purred Sheila. 'We don't want to get Hank all nervous and worked up, do we?' She moved over to a chair, picked up en article of underclothing with finger and thumb like it was a dead rat, deposited it on the bed like it was a dustbin, and sat down primly on the edge of a chair.

Cora's pert face was sullen as she glared at me. 'You didn't say anything about this dame coming,' she growled obstinately.

'Listen. Snap it up, will you?' I said desperately. 'We're late.

And she's coming. She's got to come. If she don't go, none of us goes.'

Cora's eyes flicked from me to Sheila resentfully. The article of underclothing she held draped in front of her was unwashed, the bed rumpled like it hadn't been made in days, and the room stuffy, loaded with the smell of her cheap perfume.

'What's the matter, honey,' drawled Sheila sweetly. 'Does Hank being here embarrass you?'

Sheila was far too subtle for Cora, was easily winning on points. Cora flushed angrily, was about to spit unpleasant, obscene words at Sheila, and then just managed to hold herself back. She tossed her head defiantly, said in a voice that was intended to be biting: 'I'm not worried about showing men anything. I don't have to be.'

She was right about that. And because she knew it, she proved her point. She held her head high, defiantly, held her body poised perfectly as, with a kinda exasperation, she tossed the protecting undergarment on the bed. Then, as unconcerned as though she was completely alone, she went back to painting her toe-nails.

Without knowing it, Cora had scored heavily against Sheila. Because the last thing Sheila expected was that Cora would do just what she was doing now.

It was a body blow that shook Sheila right to her toes. Sheila was sitting there on the edge of the chair with two red spots burning high up on her cheeks and red sparks burning deep down in her eyes. But it was Sheila who was humiliated now, flushed and embarrassed and taking punishment. I knew the only thing preventing her from flinging out of the room was her sheer grit and determination not to take the count.

Cora applied the finishing touches to her toenails, surveyed the results critically, was grudgingly satisfied. Much more fascinating to me was her charming unconcern about either Sheila or me.

Sheila's eyes were pinpoints of fire as Cora dug down in her wardrobe, came up with a pair of sandals.

Those sandals had very high heels, and the total effect of her long, slim, perfectly-shaped legs, emphasised by the high heels, got me sweating, dry-mouthed, open-eyed and tongue-tied.

The red-tipped toenails peeped tantalisingly through the openwork of the sandals. Cora, Sheila and I scrutinised them with widely differing reactions. Cora applied a few more deft strokes of varnish before she turned to the wardrobe, drew out the dress she'd probably selected earlier on.

It was a warm night, and it looked like it was gonna need to be. Because that dress, black, crisp and flouncy, was paper-thin. She wrestled the dress over her head, wriggled her body until the skirt fell into position around her waist, and fumbled with slender straps cunningly inserted in the bodice of the dress.

Sheila was watching intently. I was watching intently. But Cora had her back half-turned to me, and I couldn't see what was happening. Then, just as my name was trembling on Cora's lips, Sheila was out of her chair, helping Cora zip the back of the dress.

But it was when Cora turned around that I got the full effect of the dress. It was strapless and with a heart-shaped bodice. And when she faced me, I realised just how cunning had been those slender straps inside the bodice.

No brassiere could possibly have produced the same effect. Her breasts were strained high, pointed and firm, seeming to thrust at the bodice, revealing a deep, exciting cleavage that made the bodice an adornment instead of a covering.

I just couldn't take my eyes off her.

'Are you ready now?' grated Sheila, and her voice was so harsh it was unrecognisable.

I still couldn't take my eyes away from Cora.

'We're late, Hank,' grated Sheila.

I kept on looking at Cora.

Sheila stamped her foot. 'For heaven's sake, Hank. Let's get going. Let's get out of here.' There was a half-tearful entreaty in her voice now.

With an effort, I wrenched my eyes away from Cora to Sheila. There was a pained look in her eyes, a pained pleading in her face. 'It's late, Hank,' she said. 'Let's get going, shall we?'

I licked my dry lips. 'Yeah,' I said thickly. 'Let's get going.'

'I've just got to comb my hair,' said Cora, 'and then I'm ready.' Reluctantly but irresistibly, my eyes were drawn towards her. It was she who was radiant now, sensing her victory, proud and confident, almost jubilant.

She was entitled to be. She had Sheila down on the canvas taking the count.

I made another effort, turned my eyes away from Cora, looked at my watch. 'Jeepers,' I shouted. 'We're half-an-hour late already.'

'I'm coming right away,' said Cora. 'I'll finish my make-up in the car.'

9

It wasn't exactly the kinda party where you make whoopee. We were three quarters of an hour late to begin with, and dinner had been ready right on time. Our welcome was half-heartedly warm, and we were ushered almost immediately into the dining-room.

Greigs sat at the head of the table, very distinguished with his silvery hair and tuxedo. Cora ingeniously manoeuvred herself into the place at his right, and the old guy was experiencing difficulty in talking to her. He was looking at her and trying not to look at her at the same time.

Sheila sat on Greigs' left, quiet, subdued, and very beautiful in a quiet, pensive kinda way. I'd taken the seat next to Sheila, and was right opposite a guy I'd previously met: Rosa Greigs' brother, Tony Gilmore.

The other guy was there, too: the family solicitor, Warren Anderson. He stared at me stonily.

It was definitely a party that was falling flat. Greigs was trying to be charming and polite, but it was obviously only from a sense of duty for the way I'd saved his wife's life.

He'd been so anxious to steer us into the dining room, he'd even forgotten to offer us cocktails. That was a pity, because with a coupla cocktails under your belt, even the most starchy of parties begins to loosen up.

And as though Greigs could read my mind, he suddenly apologised for not serving cocktails, asked if we would like them right away.

The obvious answer that he expected was, 'No.' But a streak of obstinacy inside me asserted itself. 'Sure, that'd be a fine idea,' I said.

He gave a sickly kinda grin. 'Certainly,' he said politely. 'I should have thought of it earlier.' He gave instructions to the wooden-faced butler, pointedly instructed him to hold up the dinner for another ten minutes.

'And make the cocktails strong, huh?' I interrupted. 'Something with a bit of a kick in it, huh?'

'Certainly, certainly,' said Greigs. 'Do what Mr Janson asks,' he told the butler.

The butler took me at my word. The drink arrived in a silver-plated cocktail shaker, jade-green in colour like Sheila's eyes, and iced. There was a full glass for everyone, and the drink had a kick like the take-off impetus of an atomic rocket.

It was interesting to note everyone's reactions. Greigs took a tiny sip at his glass, put it down with an expressionless face. Tony Gilmore gulped at his, rolled the liquid around his tongue approvingly. Anderson's nostrils quivered apprehensively as he raised the glass to his lips. He sipped warily, replaced the glass on the table in front of him with his nostrils still quivering like a terrier scenting a rat.

Cora gulped half her cocktail in one go, sighed deliciously, leaned forward with her elbows on the table and looked up into Greigs' face. The way she was sitting, bent forward, enabled him to explore the full depths of the cleavage with his eyes. And when a girl like Cora sets out to make an impression, boy, she makes an impression.

She made an impression on Greigs. He was hypnotised, couldn't take his eyes off her.

And Sheila?

Quiet, ladylike and reserved, she drank her cocktail in gentle sips. She replaced the half-empty glass on the table, smiled across at Anderson politely.

I gulped my cocktail, wished I hadn't been so smart in asking the butler to give it a kick. It had four kicks now. Four kicks all booting me at the same time. Right in the belly. That cocktail was a sizzler. And while I tried to appear nonchalant and keep my face expressionless, I was mentally taking my hat off to Sheila for her facial control.

Because that cocktail was making my hair stand on end, burning my throat, seeping down inside me like molten lead, sending fiery tongues of hot fumes licking up around my brain.

That cocktail was a scorcher!

'And how is your wife now?' Cora was saying, and she was leaning towards Greigs, looking up into his face, with a sweet, melancholy expression that made her look like an innocent young dame not yet out of high school.

He looked at her, peered down into the subtle shadows of the cleavage, cleared his throat, and said hoarsely: 'Much better, my dear. Much better.'

'I'm so pleased,' purred Cora, and she moved subtly. Her bosom moved at the same time, the creamy whiteness seeming possessed of a life and vitality of its own.

'Nice of you to say so, my dear,' said Greigs, and his voice was hoarse and strained. He reached quickly for his cocktail, gulped half of it like water before he remembered what a kick it had. I fancied I could see his silvery hairs beginning to prick.

The spike of Sheila's high heel found my toes, ground savagely.

I suppressed a grunt of pain, found Sheila smiling at me sweetly. 'I'm here, too, honey,' she said.

'I know, honey,' I replied softly, grinding my teeth. 'Did you want something?' I added under my breath: 'If you start anything here, I'll tear you in little pieces.'

'You haven't introduced me, honey,' she drawled. 'You haven't told Mr Greigs who I really am.'

I stared at her. 'You want me to tell him?'

'Of course,' she said, reprovingly. 'I'm Mr Greigs' guest. I don't want to be here under false pretences.'

I cleared my throat, reached for my cocktail, finished it. When the hot fumes had ceased scorching my brain, I cleared my throat again, said softly: 'One moment, please, Mr Greigs.'

The old guy was completely out of his depth. He hadn't a chance. Cora had his eyes on a string and irresistibly drawn towards her. A momentary look of irritation crossed his face as he turned towards me.

'I've already introduced Sheila Lang,' I commenced. 'But I didn't mention she is also employed by the *Chronicle*.'

'Very nice, my dear,' he said absently, nodding his head. 'I'm sure your work must be most interesting.'

I caught him as he was turning back to Cora.

'I should explain,' I added, 'that Miss Lang hopes while she is here to combine business with pleasure.'

A puzzled frown puckered his forehead. 'Business with pleasure?'

'Miss Lang,' I explained, slowly and carefully, 'is editoress of the woman's page of the *Chicago Chronicle*. It seems that her readers are interested in the Roman utensils that have recently been discovered, and that you are at present examining. Miss Lang was hoping you will be good enough to give her an interview on this subject.'

He didn't like it. His frown intensified, his eyes became hard, and his lips tightened. He took a deep breath, said slowly: 'I have never been a man to wish to publicise myself and ...'

Cora saved the situation. She said, with a delighted exclamation: 'Oh, do tell, Mr Greigs. It's all so terribly exciting. I've been reading about it in the *Chicago Chronicle*. Just think of all those beautiful things discovered after being buried for more than two thousand years, and today exactly as they were all that time ago. They say there's bottles of perfume with the perfume still inside them. It must be terribly thrilling!'

Greigs' eyes turned to Cora, and inevitably they lowered. 'Are you really interested, my dear?' he said, and there was just the faintest note of doubt in his voice, mingled with pleased surprise.

'I'm crazy to hear more about it,' she said excitedly, and impulsively reached out, took his hand.

His voice was faint. 'I never thought ...' he said. 'I mean ... the younger generation, I thought, weren't interested in these things.'

'The younger generation,' echoed Cora, with a note of surprise in her voice. 'Why do you say that?'

'It's obvious, my dear. There's such a difference in our ages.'

Her eyes were tender and innocent, staring up into his with a softness that was difficult to believe was artificial. 'I never thought of you as being old,' she said softly, and her fingers were smoothing the back of his hand.

He couldn't have believed her. But he wanted to. He sighed blissfully, reached for his cocktail, finished it before he replaced the glass. And if you've ever seen an old guy smile bashfully, you'll know just how stupid and fatuous he can appear.

Warren Anderson drew out a large white handkerchief, trumpeted into it with a noise that was more like a gigantic snort than a dinner table gesture.

Tony Gilmore had finished his cocktail, was busy pouring the remaining dregs of the cocktail shaker into his own glass. He hadn't the slightest interest in anything that was going on.

And Cora was still working on Greigs. She had his bony hand between both of hers now, arching her back achingly as she strained to thrust her breasts up towards him.

I leaned slightly sideways so I could whisper in Sheila's ear. 'Round two goes to Cora.'

She glared at me balefully. 'What on earth are you talking about?'

She knew damned well what I was talking about. I shrugged my shoulders. 'None of it's my business, anyway. I merely brought you here. That's what you wanted, isn't it? From this point onwards, you're on your own.'

She said, in a low undertone: 'Just keep out of my hair, Hank. Just keep outta my hair.'

There was something different about the party atmosphere. There was less tenseness, less frigidity, a kinda, warm, human feeling spreading through the room, like everyone was melting.

That was when I knew the cocktails had been a grand idea. And though we'd kept the dinner waiting, there was nothing to complain of. In truth, the dinner was perfect. And to complete the perfection was the wine that was served with it. Good vintage wine, decanted correctly and with a wonderful bouquet.

I felt warm and satisfied with life when the fruit plates were cleared away by the butler and black coffee was served. Brandy was poured into large glasses, warmed at the table in the flame of a mentholated spirits stove.

Yeah, it was a perfect meal, and I was feeling good. And glancing around the table, it seemed to me there were only two people who didn't feel good. One was Sheila, sitting beside me as stiff as a ramrod, her cheeks still slightly flushed and staring fixedly at her brandy glass. The other was Warren Anderson, puffing hard on a cigar with an untouched wine glass in front of him and his brandy looking like it was also going to be neglected.

There was no doubting that Tony Gilmore was happy. He hadn't said a word to anyone, and didn't look as though he had the time or inclination to do so. He'd been eating and drinking steadily, without once pausing to speak. Now he was sitting back in his chair with a contented smile on his face, cuddling the brandy glass and with at least half a bottle of wine warming his belly.

Greigs was a gonna. He'd drunk more wine than an old guy his age should drink. And apart from that, he was a gonna. He'd edged his chair around closer to Cora and was now shamelessly caressing her smoothly rounded arms.

Cora was happy. By that, I mean she had the look of a dame who is completely successful. But it was acting. Because no dame, no matter how mercenary, could get a kick out of being mauled that way by an old guy like Greigs. But the drink had brought a flush to her cheeks, given a sparkle to her eyes, made her radiant. And with that warm wine and brandy-inspired glow inside me, after looking at the Sphinx-like, ice-cold Sheila beside me and then across the table at the hot, vital, warm-blooded Cora, I knew which side of the table I wanted to be sitting.

It was Greigs who upset the brandy. He moved his arm quickly, carelessly, sent the glass sprawling, the brandy trickling across the virgin whiteness of the tablecloth, dripping onto Cora's lap.

Immediately he was all attention, on his feet, dabbing at her with his napkin. Meanwhile Cora was protesting it was nothing at all, that it really didn't matter, that it was an accident and couldn't be helped, and that he shouldn't upset himself.

I knew she was figuring the least she was gonna get out of this was a new dress.

That accident kinda broke up the dinner party. Greigs took Cora's arm, held on to it tightly. The old coot was so far gone by this time, he hadn't even the sense to think about his wife's brother. Not that Tony Gilmore was interested anyway.

Greigs said: 'What shall we do now, my dear? Do you play bridge, canasta, or are you interested in music? Whatever you say.'

Cora switched on a pained loot of surprise. 'But you promised, Greigs,' she said. 'I do so want to see those Roman relics.'

'Of course, my dear, how stupid of me. You shall see them at once.' Addressing everyone, he said: 'I suppose you would all like to see them.'

I grunted.

Sheila said quietly: 'I would indeed, Mr Greigs.'

'If you'll come this way, then,' he said, and took an even firmer grip on Cora's arm, led the way out of the dining room and up the wide, thickly carpeted staircase.

Sheila pinched my elbow as we followed him. 'What's she after?' she demanded fiercely. 'Why is she making a play for the old goat?'

I glanced over my shoulder quickly. Gilmore and Anderson were following us. Tony Gilmore didn't look as though he knew why he was trailing along, but Anderson was on his toes, his eyes sharp and piercing. There wasn't the slightest doubt he'd heard every word Sheila spoke.

'She just likes him, I guess,' I said lamely.

Sheila's finger and thumb nipped and twisted my flesh. 'If you're holding out on me, you big ape,' she threatened ominously.

'Cut it out, will you, Scallywag,' I growled. 'I don't know any more about her than you do.'

We'd reached the top of the staircase by now. We followed Greigs along a wide, thickly-carpeted corridor, flanked with marble busts of famous composers.

'And here, my dear,' Greigs said, opening up double doors leading into a huge room lined with books, 'is my study.' There was just the faintest trace of pride in his voice.

It sure was some study, and with all the books he had at his disposal, given enough time, a guy could write a complete history of the world.

'Of course,' said Greigs, taking a fresh grip on Cora's arm and peering down into the cleavage, 'you must realise you are greatly privileged. These relics are priceless.'

He crossed to his desk, fumbled beneath it, operated a switch. He tittered a little tipsily. 'A gadget of mine,' he smirked. 'A burglar alarm which operates when anyone touches the safe.'

Cora's eyes were wide and wondering. 'They're really terribly valuable, these relics?'

'Of course, my dear. We must take great care of them.' He was moving to the corner of the room now, and from the corner of my eye I saw Anderson make a half movement of protest and then let his arm drop back to his side. He shrugged his shoulders as though to say. *'It's none of my business, anyway.'*

The wall safe was cunningly concealed. Nobody would have found it without taking the room apart, unless Greigs had shown them. He showed us. He was as pleased as a child at the way it worked. He showed us two or three times, applied pressure to three separate books at the same time so that a whole bank of books swung away from the wall, revealing a large combination safe.

But Greigs had just enough caution left inside him to keep his head and shoulders between us and the safe while he twirled the dials, set them and jerked it open. He forgot however that when the door of the safe swung open we could see all the dials.

Allowing no-one else to touch the contents of the safe, carrying them as reverently as though they were priceless treasures – as indeed they were – he brought the relics to the table one by one, deposited them carefully like he was displaying the crown jewels.

Personally, I never find things are any the more beautiful because they are old. I'd rather have a Luger any day than the stone axe of a pre-historic man. But there's always a touch of romance attached to an article that has existed for untold generations.

For example, the perfume flask that Greigs deposited carefully on the table. Glass-making in Roman days wasn't the highly skilled and scientific industry it is today. The flask was conical-shaped, the glass obscured and tinted with mother-of-pearl colourings. Inside was a light blue liquid of a shade I didn't think I had ever before encountered.

Cora stared at it with eyes wide and shining. 'And is it really a perfume that is more than two thousand years old?'

Now that he was displaying these treasures, almost fondling them, Greigs was losing some of his haziness and regaining his scholarly lust for knowledge. He said, cautiously: 'That I'm not prepared to say at the moment. There are a number of factors that have to be taken into consideration. It will need some weeks of study before I am able to declare with reasonable certainty from which epoch these relics have come. I can be reasonably sure, however, my dear, that we can place it approximately at five hundred years before Christ.

Her little mouth rounded in an O of surprise.

Sheila, crisply and efficiently, produced her notebook.

'Would you say that the Romans' knowledge of glass-blowing was a comparatively new innovation at that time, or did they possess the knowledge for some considerable time without improving upon it.'

Greigs cleared his throat, started answering.

I let his river of words wash over me unnoticed as my mind drifted back along the road of time, following the trail of a tiny, delicate flask of perfume back to the hands of a Roman mistress of the house. I imagined her in a marble-columned and velvet-draped sleeping chamber, seated at the Roman equivalent of a dressing table, while scantily-clothed handmaidens carefully brushed her long hair and applied sweet-smelling oils to her body.

And now imagined beauty and splendour was all that remained of a vast Empire.

There were many other articles of interest: earrings carved from bone and copper, crudely fashioned metal forks scarred with the erosion of time, an earthenware wine flagon, a bone salt cellar, an earthenware platter, bone fishing hooks, and a dozen other articles that proved the Roman way of life had not been so very much different from our way of life two thousand years later.

Meanwhile, Anderson was watching the items displayed on the table with the eye of a vulture, almost as though he suspected one of us might try to slip an article into our pockets.

And now Greigs was warming to his favourite subject of ancient history, was forgetting Cora and diverting his attention to Sheila, who with quiet, sober eyes was listening intelligently and noting everything he said.

I could see the anger glinting in Cora's eyes. She took Greigs' arm, linked her fingers in his, squeezed.

He went on talking to Sheila.

Cora swayed herself against him so that her hip rested against his. He faltered momentarily, went on talking to Sheila.

Quite openly and brazenly, Cora nudged his elbow with her breast.

He terminated his sentence with difficulty, mopped his forehead, looked at Cora and said, huskily: 'Excuse me neglecting you, my dear. I'm afraid I got carried away.'

'I think they're simply ducky,' Cora said, smiling sweetly. 'But we have spent rather a long time with them, don't you think?'

'Of course,' he said at once, visibly melting under her charm.

Gently, tenderly, he gathered up the relics and replaced

them carefully in the safe under the watchful eye of Warren Anderson, who appeared to be checking every item. I guess solicitors just are that way, can't help it.

Meanwhile, Tony Gilmore had found a brandy bottle and was seated at the far end of the library. He hadn't once glanced at the relics, instead was gazing dreamily at the bottom of the glass through two inches of brandy.

'I shall have to start work on these tomorrow,' said Greigs, as he closed the safe door, twirled the combination dials and concealed it behind the bank of books.

Soft-footed, Warren Anderson crossed to the desk, fumbled underneath it, and I heard the click of the switch as he reset the burglar alarm.

We all made a move towards the door, Cora once again grabbing Greigs' arm and hanging on to it like it was a lifebelt.

We were halfway along the corridor when I asked him about his wife.

'Oh, yes, of course,' he said absently. 'Would you like to see her for a minute?' He peered at me anxiously, as if he wouldn't hear my reply unless his eyes were watching my lips.

'I don't want to disturb her ...' I began.

'Please do,' he insisted. 'I'd like you to see her.'

The bedroom was a few paces away from the library. He opened the door quietly, beckoned us inside. Cora and I slid inside, soft-footed.

A middle-aged, private nurse, wearing a crisp, starched, white uniform was reading quietly in the dim light of a table-lamp. Rosa Greigs was sleeping peacefully, a faint flush of health on her cheeks and her breathing soft and normal.

The nurse raised her finger to her lips warningly, gestured us not to disturb her.

Cora, Greigs and I stood staring at Rosa Greigs for maybe half a minute. I nodded at Greigs to show I thought his wife looked much better, left the room quietly, followed by Greigs and Cora.

'You see, she's very much better now,' Greigs said, as he closed the door behind him.

'Does she still …' I broke off, unwilling to finish the sentence.

'No,' he said, and his old eyes were suddenly worried. 'There hasn't been any more trouble. If she rests for a few more weeks, the doctors are certain she will improve rapidly.'

'The nurse is reliable?' I asked.

'Thoroughly reliable,' he said, and his fingers were locking with Cora's again as she looped her arm in his.

'Watches her day and night, I suppose?' I persisted.

'She's much better now,' he told me. 'We have two nurses taking turns to be with her during the day. Rosa has a sleeping draught at night, and we lock the door until the following morning.'

Sheila was listening with wide open eyes. Greigs noticed her expression, said anxiously: 'None of this is for publication, of course.'

I took Sheila by the arm, gouged my fingers hard. 'You heard what the gentleman said,' I rasped. 'This isn't for publication. Understand?'

She wrenched her arm away fiercely. 'I heard,' she snarled.

Greigs said, anxiously: 'But my dear, I do plead with you. Please don't report anything you've just learned.'

Sheila looked at him steadily. 'I'm your guest, Mr Greigs,' she said sincerely. 'I was very pleased to have your opinion about the Roman relics, and I most certainly shall not abuse your hospitality by prying into your private life.'

We'd reached the bottom of the stairs by this time and, suddenly remembering his duties as host, Greigs asked abruptly: 'What would you like to do now? Music, or a drink or is there any …'

'Poker!' said Cora, excited and eager. 'Let's play poker.'

Greigs looked doubtful. 'I'm not sure I know how …'

'Never mind, darling,' she said eagerly. 'You'll soon learn.'

She was hugging his arm, her fingers fondling his. Inevitably his eyes were drawn to the vigorous thrust of her firmly moulded breasts. 'I'm sure you'll be an excellent teacher,' he said, and the old fella simpered sickeningly.

Five of us played, while Gilmore sat in a nearby armchair,

happily contented with another glass of brandy. We played a few experimental rounds until Greigs got the hang of the game. Meanwhile, the butler reported that the nurse had left. Mrs Greigs was sleeping quietly.

We began playing for small stakes, and much to my surprise, Cora, instead of having incredible luck, or alarming skill, began to lose steadily. The stakes were low and weren't going to break anyone. But after a time, Cora wanted to get her handbag from my car to make sure she had enough to pay her losses.

I offered to stake her.

She refused charmingly but with finality. She also refused to let me get her bag for her.

I gave her the key of my car, and we all sat back and waited. She was absent some time, and I was on the point of going to look for her when she hurried in, smiling ruefully and describing how she'd dropped the car key in the dark and couldn't find it. Then we had to wait again while Cora went upstairs to powder her face.

We played for another hour, during which time nearly everyone, including Greigs himself, was absent from the room for a few minutes for some reason or another.

And then, just when the game was getting really interesting, with the stakes mounting up in one of the biggest bluffs that so far had been made, we were all suddenly startled by the abrupt slamming of the front door.

Andersen's head went up, his ears prickling like a startled rabbit's, his hands frozen in mid-air in the act of dropping more dimes in the kitty. Greigs and Tony Gilmore stared at each other in consternation.

I sensed their numbed reaction, asked quickly: 'There's no way she could have got out, is there?

'Let's go see,' Anderson said, suddenly brisk and alert.

Greigs was out of his chair then so quickly it skeetered backwards, toppled with a crash. Anderson was already out through the door, bounding up the stairs like a mountain goat. Greigs, despite his age, was close behind me as I ran for the main door, wrenched it open.

'Where would she go?' I rasped. 'What would she be likely to do?'

'The garage,' he panted. 'The car. That's the first thing she'd make for.'

Anderson was at the top of the stairs behind us, his voice loaded with alarm. 'It's her,' he shouted. 'Her door's unlocked. She must have got out.'

'Where's the garage?' I rasped.

'Round to the right,' panted Greigs. 'I'll show you.' He led the way as quickly as he could go, half-walking, half-running.

It was hopeless. We heard the hum of the engine long before we could reach the garage, saw the headlights spring into life, cleave through the darkness to outline the open driveway, winding down towards the main drag.

She'd got the car rolling, the soft purr of the engine blasting into a savage roar as she rammed her foot down on the gas. It was a powerful car, capable of high speeds. A car of that calibre deliberately driven against a brick wall would reduce the driver to a red smear.

On foot, there was no chance of reaching her. But there was another way, a slender hope that she could be stopped before she reached the main drag.

I fumbled in my pocket for my car key as I ran madly towards my own car parked the other side of the driveway.

My fingers were all thumbs. In the darkness, I couldn't get the key into the door handle to unlock the car. And when I did and turned the key, the car was still locked, showing that Cora had left the car unlocked and I'd wasted valuable time re-locking it.

I got the door open, thrust myself inside, inserting the ignition key in the dashboard with one hand while I frantically felt for the brake handle with the other.

My car always starts first try with no trouble. Maybe I was over-anxious, in too much of a hurry. I had to thumb the self-starter three times before the engine burst into life.

Then it was a matter of seconds. I knew that once Mrs Greigs was out on the main drag, I'd never catch her, not before she'd done what she wanted to do, anyway. I slammed through the gears and tramped on the gas. My headlights cut a white swathe through the night, and I saw her a third of the way down the drive, rolling at speed, tyres screeching as she took the asphalt curves of the drive at too high a speed.

There was just one slender chance I could stop her. I hated like hell to take it, but there was no alternative.

I clenched my teeth, slammed into top gear and felt my car wheels bump up over the grass verge.

10

There was only one way I could make up the distance she'd gained. The drive was winding like a snake through the lawns and flower beds. By driving straight as the crow flies, I could cut down her lead, maybe reach her before she reached the entrance gates.

And even as I ploughed across flower beds, felt my wheels churn soft earth, bump off the grass verge onto the drive, only to feel the steering wheel jolt in my hands as I once again bumped up on to the grass verge, there was still room in my mind for conflicting emotions.

I was proud of my car, proud of its slender lines, its perfect performance and its smoothness of action. It was a car to be handled with kid gloves. Driving it over rough ground like I was doing, scraping the wings with brambles and bushes, punishing the suspension with savage bumping, gave me almost a physical pain.

And mingled with my disgust at the necessity of the damage to my car, was a bitter hatred of Cora. Because it was all so clear now. Going out to my car had been an excuse to cover up her going upstairs to unlock the door of Mrs Greigs' room. Cora had given that poor woman just one more opportunity to kill herself. And anger flamed high inside me. Because Cora hadn't done this thing off her own bat. She'd involved me, induced me to get an invitation to Greigs' house so she could do this thing!

And all the time these confused thoughts were running riot

in my mind, I was rocketing across the ground at an ever-increasing speed, my sweaty hands slippery on the steering wheel, my wrists aching with the strain of fighting the savage wrenching and twisting of the steering wheel, which writhed like a live thing in my hands.

And now, as our two sets of headlights rushed through the darkness towards the entrance gates, I calculated I could just about make it. I could reach the entrance gates just about the same time as she did.

It wasn't any answer to the problem. I still had to stop her! And there was just one way to do it. A method that made me go cold, made me sick at the belly.

But I had to do it, because once she passed through those gates, nothing would stop her.

I was overtaking her fast now, both of us on the straight for the entrance gates, screaming along side by side with my bonnet edging up level with her back wheels. I hooted loudly and automatically, instinctively, she pulled over, allowed me to draw up level with the driving seat. Then the two of us were hurtling together towards the entrance gates, and they were almost wide enough for two cars to pass through side by side. Almost.

But not quite!

In the last few seconds, she musta realised we couldn't get through the gates together. I was hoping like hell she'd act instinctively. Slam on her brakes, drag her car to a halt.

But she didn't!

It was a matter of feet now, and a matter of seconds. I gritted my teeth, swung my car towards her, locked hubs with her so that side by side we rocketed towards the brick gateway.

The grinding, the wrenching and tearing of metal was a torturous destruction of my brain and heart. As my car was pinched to a standstill, crushed side by side in the gateway with the other car, I «aw my beautiful streamlined wings concertinaing, metal peeling away from the side of my car like an orange being skinned.

I sat for seconds, gouging my nails into the palms of my

hands, listening to the final dying sounds of broken, twisted metal settling down into the horrifying silence that immediately follows an accident.

But there was still Rosa Greigs to think about. She'd already despaired of opening the jammed front door, was clambering over into the back seat to force open the back door.

To lose her now, after sacrificing my car, would be just too much. I launched myself over the seat into the back of the car. The back door was jammed, wouldn't open more than a coupla inches. I sweated, strained, managed to force it another few inches.

I took the skin off my face, my shoulder and my hip, wrestling myself through that narrow slit just in time to glimpse her running into the belt of trees that flanked the walls of the grounds.

There was a quarter moon filtered by flakes of cloud. It enabled me to get a glimpse of her from time to time as I went after her like a greyhound scenting a hare, overtaking her just about as easily.

I was within five yards of her when my foot caught a root. I was running all out, unsuspecting. I hit the ground with my face, chest and knees all at the same time. The fall knocked the breath out of me, and I'd almost lost sight of her by the time I'd climbed to my feet again. And now blood was trickling down my face, running down into my eye from a bad cut just over the eyebrow.

I gritted my teeth, jabbed my elbows into my sides, set off after her.

I'd never have thought a woman of thirty-five could have had so much go in her. She was in and out of those trees like quicksilver. Maybe she could see better than me, because I kept barking my shins on tree branches, stumbling on rough ground, running my head into trailing creepers.

But I caught her at last, flung one arm around her waist, grasped her shoulder detainingly.

She reacted with unexpected violence, buried her teeth in my hand, and as I shouted with the pain of it, kicked out at me savagely.

But now I'd got her, nothing was gonna make me lose her. I pulled my hand free from her teeth, feeling flesh rend at the same time. Then I got a firm grip on her, arms clamped behind her back, and standing with my legs astride so that she couldn't back-heel my shins.

She'd used up almost all her energy in that final, frantic attempt at freedom. She broke suddenly, became limp and trembling, non-resisting and pathetic. Her shoulders shook as she wept silently, huge sobs that welled up from deep down inside her, shook her from head to toe, sobs that were unnatural, born of nervous hysteria.

Gently I put my arm around her, led her back across the grounds to the lights of the house. Already the others were looking for us, searching with flashlamps. When I got near enough, I shouted to them, and they came running, worried and anxious.

Tony Gilmore was the first to reach me. He shone his flashlamp on us, said in a voice of great relief: 'Thank God you've found her.'

Right behind him was Greigs, panting asthmatically, shaking in his anxiety and concern.

Sheila shouldered me to one side with a smooth, efficient air. 'Okay, Hank,' she said quietly. 'Let me take care of her. She needs a woman's sympathy.'

'She's really all right, not hurt?' quavered Greigs, his voice loaded with concern.

'Sure, she's okay,' I said. 'She may be a little exhausted from running. But she's okay.'

Cora stood beside Greigs, took his arm affectionately. 'Don't get too upset about her,' she said. 'Women do get hysterical at times, you know.'

Her cool, innocent voice curdled the anger inside me. I was remembering my smashed, wrecked car and Cora's cold-blooded, merciless greed. It was all I could do to prevent myself tearing her away from Greigs, burying my thumbs deep in her windpipe until her eyes spurted from her head.

But that would come later. The important thing was to get Rosa Greigs back to her house.

Sheila led the way, with Tony Gilmore holding the torch. Sheila was talking quietly, consolingly, and was having a soothing effect on Mrs Greigs, whose weeping was gently ebbing.

Greigs muttered distractedly: 'I couldn't bear it if anything happened to her.'

'Of course not,' said Cora sympathetically. 'But she's going to be all right. Don't you worry.'

Once again I had to struggle to keep my temper under control. Maybe I wouldn't have managed it if Anderson and the butler, who were running to meet us, had not arrived at that moment.

Anderson burst out agitatedly: 'The relics, Greigs, the relics!'

I'd mentally docketed Anderson as a guy who never gets excited about anything. But he was sure excited now, almost dancing in agitation.

'What about the relics?' asked Greigs disinterestedly, obviously concerned about Rosa.

'They're gone,' shouted Anderson. 'They've been stolen. Stolen!'

There was a kinda stunned silence. I shouldered Greigs to one side, pushed close to Anderson, thrust my face close against his. 'What do you mean, stolen?' I demanded.

'They're gone,' he said nervously, agitatedly. 'The safe door's open, the window's open and the safe's cleaned out.'

The butler was too old a man to run around that way, He was puffing like a locomotive. 'It's true,' he panted. 'The safe's been emptied.'

'We must search for them,' said Anderson excitedly. 'They must be around somewhere. The robbery's only just taken place.'

'How d'you know?' I rasped.

The butler said, pantingly: 'I looked in the library twenty minutes ago to lock up for the night. Everything was all right then.'

'Listen, man,' I rasped. 'When you locked up, was that window already bolted, or was it unbolted.'

He thought. 'It was unbolted.'

'The guy was probably already in the house, hiding in the library while you were bolting the window through which he entered,' I guessed.

Greigs' face was white in the reflection of the flashlamps. 'This is terrible,' he croaked. 'This is simply terrible. We must get the police at once.'

'Forget the police now,' I rasped. 'There's a chance the thief's still in the grounds somewhere. Sheila and Cora, you get Mrs Greigs up to the house. The rest of you spread out, cover as much ground as you can. If you see or hear anything, give a loud shout, a really loud shout. The rest of us will come running immediately. Get it?'

'Look after my wife, my dear,' urged Greigs.

'She'll be all right with me,' said Sheila, and there was a quiet, reassuring confidence in her voice.

Cora went around the other side of Rosa Greigs, held her arm. 'She'll be all right,' she promised. 'We'll take great care of her.'

I felt the red tide of anger brimming high inside me. I grated in a hoarse voice: 'Sheila!'

She looked over her shoulder at me.

'Don't leave Mrs Greigs,' I said warningly. 'Whatever happens, don't leave her for one minute.

'Don't leave her,' I repeated warningly.

There was a note in my voice that warned Sheila this was something special. She said, quietly: 'All right, Hank. You can leave it with me.' The way she said it, I knew I could rely on her.

'All right everyone,' I rasped loudly. 'Split up. Gilmore and Anderson, as far over to the left as you can go. Greigs and the butler, you take the central section here. I'll take the right. Start walking towards the house, and at the slightest sound or sight of anything, give a loud yell so everyone can come running.'

They split up, vanished into the dusk like grey ghosts.

I knew it was as good as hopeless. There was just one chance in a hundred thousand the thief was still in the grounds. But that chance might come off. I threaded my way through trees, across lawns, turned softly, and listened carefully for any tiny sound.

The moonlight was fitful, at times penetrating the clouds and at other times completely obscured, leaving me in darkness.

At the end of twenty minutes, I hadn't got anywhere, and it didn't look to me like I was gonna get anywhere either. I took a cigarette from my pack, carefully shielded the lighter with my hand as I lit up. I stood there, puffing the red glow of my cigarette into life and trying to parallel the thief's thinking processes.

The set-up worried me. It was all too pat. The thief had to know about the burglar alarm and how the safe was hidden. That meant he had to have inside knowledge. And it stunk.

The whole set-up was too pat, too smooth and too easy. Almost like everything had been carefully pre-arranged, culminating in the escape of Rosa Greigs, undercover of which the thief had his chance to make a getaway.

The more I thought about it, the more it stunk.

Once again I drew on my cigarette. The moon had disappeared behind heavy clouds, and the red, glowing end of my cigarette spread a momentary reflection that showed my face.

It didn't make much more noise than an air-gun. Not at all frightening, except for the spang of lead boring the air above my head.

It shook me. It shook me right down to my heels, caused my heart to take a great leap.

This time the guy was using a silencer, and this time he oughtn't to have missed. He'd been trying so long now, the mathematical odds were now in his favour for scoring a bull.

But it didn't follow that the more he tried, the more I became accustomed to being a target. It wasn't quick thinking that made me jerk my cigarette in one direction and throw myself bodily backwards in the opposite direction.

It was shock and fear!

Shock that made my muscles contract and my throat dry. Fear that caused a crazy, gibbering spectre to rear up at the roots of my brain and urge me to run blindly, crazily, madly; run anywhere that would take me away from the imminent threat of death.

But I didn't run. And it wasn't because I wasn't afraid. It was because some inner, sane instinct held me back, impressed on my consciousness that the sound of footsteps would give away my position, might easily buy me a bullet between the shoulder blades.

I lay still, not breathing, listening to the awful hammering of my heart that seemed to resound and echo right to the distant hills.

I listened above the sound of the pumping of my heart to the silence.

Just silence.

Then the faint rustle of the trees, the furry movement of tiny things scuttling through the night, the distant sad cry of a bird and the rustle of a falling pine cone.

I couldn't hear him, but he was still there.

I knew he was there, with the sure instinct that I knew death was but a few short paces away.

I lay still, quite still. As still as the grave.

He was as motionless as me, waiting, listening and determined, his gun heavy in his hand and his eyes piercing the cloak of the darkness to find his prey.

An inch at a time, I moved my arm, wriggled my fingers around and into my pocket, gently drew out my cigarette pack. It caught in the coat lining, and I spent anxious moments releasing it.

I tensed myself, flexed every muscle for the sudden, rapid movement I must make. Then, with my screaming nerves balancing on a razor-edge, I poised the cigarette pack, sent it skimming as far away from me into the darkness as I could throw it.

In that eerie, waiting silence, it made a deafening noise and it hit the ground. And this time, as lead whirred I saw the spurt of flame maybe twenty-five yards away from me. I was on my feet running, then, running zigzag towards the blotch of flame.

I shoulda known he'd be sheltering among the trees. I threw myself to one side just in time, jagged my shoulder against one tree, blundered into another.

Again lead spat, and this time I heard the chunky sound of lead burying itself in wood a few feet away from me. But now I was under cover of the trees, and it made all the difference. I bent carefully, gathered up a handful of pine cones. He musta caught the faint sound of my movements because lead plunked into the other side of the tree. I tossed the pine cones as hard as I could, one after the other, all in the same direction, placing them at intervals to give the impression of somebody running in that direction.

It worked!

He used two more bullets, and as the silencer spat for the sixth time, I heaved a sigh of relief.

Because the scores were even now. I didn't think he'd carry a gun that fired more than six shots without reloading. And of one thing I was quite sure.

I wasn't going to give that guy a chance to reload!

I ran towards the last spurt of gunfire, and momentarily the moon gleamed through a rift in the cloud. I saw him then, a moonshaft flitting across his shoulders as he plunged in among the trees.

I kept right on after him. This time, I was gonna get him. I was boiling mad. The shock reaction of lead spitting at me had keyed my nerves to flash point. I wanted to get my hands on that guy, mash his face with my fists, beat him to a jelly.

He sure knew how to run. Every time I stopped to listen, he seemed to be heading a different direction, and each time he sounded further away.

I gritted my teeth, plunged on determinedly. I found there was a very real fear inside me now, the fear he might escape me and that there might be another time when he wouldn't miss.

Again I stopped and listened, and there was real anxiety inside me now. Because now I couldn't hear him at all. I waited a few seconds, moved on slowly, softly, ears cocked all the time, waiting for a slight sound to give me a lead.

And now that gibbering fear was gnawing at the back of my brain again, causing my hairs to prick. Because the unseen killer was getting another chance, getting an opportunity to reload.

Every nerve in my body was keyed to snapping point. My ears were cocked for every slight sound, and I was holding my breath, listening to my heart pounding like a steam hammer.

And then I heard it!

A tiny scuffling sound coming, surprisingly, from the opposite direction to that I expected.

I moved in towards the sound. It came again, much more distinctly this time, followed by the sharp snapping of a twig. He was quite close; not more than fifteen feet away.

Maybe he'd got that gun reloaded, maybe not. There was only one line of action left to me. I launched myself towards the sound.

He hadn't reloaded, because he didn't blast at me. Instead he broke cover, blundered frantically away from me, as the moon broke through the clouds, glinted across his shoulders.

I was right behind him, swerving, plunging, avoiding tree roots and steadily overhauling him.

He wasn't thinking. I was outrunning him, and he had more chance among the trees. But he didn't stick to the trees. He broke out into the open, put on a burst of speed that momentarily put him a coupla yards ahead.

This guy had been slinging lead at me so long, he'd got me as jumpy as a barefooted man on tin-tacks. He wasn't gonna get away this time.

I summoned my strength, pumped my legs twice as fast in a sudden, final spurt that brought me level with him. I flung myself at him full length in a rugby tackle, wrapped my arms around his knees, brought him crashing to the ground.

He kicked out madly, planted one heel in my chest, and the other in the centre of my forehead. That was rough play, and I didn't like it. I half-rose, half-fell on him again, this time my knees together and pointing. The air went out of him with a whoosh, my knees punching his belly so hard they almost hit his spine. And while he was still choking, I swung up and along the length of his body, planted my knuckles so cleanly beneath his chin that the pain of it shocked my arm to the shoulder.

But there was still plenty of fight in him. He jagged his knees up high towards his chest, nearly took my groin along with them.

I sweated, felt myself go faint with pain, held on grimly to consciousness as I spreadeagled myself on him, my weight holding him down.

He had yet another trick up his sleeve. His head jerked up, butted me twice beneath the chin, snapping my teeth together with such force I felt them crumbling.

He was a tough boy who wanted to fight the tough way. I could be tough, too, when necessary. And I was so sick with pain, I wasn't overmuch preoccupied with being a gentleman.

It was a trick he didn't know and had probably never heard of. He was rigid with agony, a screech of pain crackling in his throat. Meanwhile, I used my elbow, jagged it again, hard, deep down into his solar plexus, like I was trying to dig a hole in him.

He was sobbing with pain, and all the fight knocked outta him as I straddled his chest, knelt on his upper arms, crooked my finger around his throat.

'Fella, you have asked for this,' I rasped, and there was a red haze of anger clouding my head so that I knew I was gonna have to exert control if I wasn't gonna kill him.

He gurgled, gasped, and his hands came up to encircle mine, try to wrench them from his throat. I loosed one hand from his neck, smacked his face with the flat of my palm so hard I almost lifted his head off his shoulders. Then I slapped in the other direction to bring his head back straight again.

He groaned piteously.

I didn't have any pity left in me. I swiped him again, felt a flood of savage satisfaction wash over me when his lips split and blood spurted against my knuckles.

The hot stickiness of his blood on my knuckles aroused within me a kinda animal-like hunger. This guy had been stalking me, these last few days, scaring me to death and ruthlessly killing a sweet young dame who didn't know what it was all about.

I swiped him once more, and this time his body arched up in pain, nearly throwing me off his chest.

'This is just the beginning,' I gritted. 'You're really going to get a work-out, fella.'

The light of a flashlamp spat out from the darkness, bathed us in a white halo. With my fist upraised, I blinked up into the sharp white light, trying to see who was holding it.

Cora said in a tight, controlled little voice: 'For God's sake, Hank. Leave him alone.'

'Keep out of this,' I warned. 'This guy's dangerous. Just watch yourself.'

She kinda sprang at me, fingers gouging into my shoulders. She snarled frantically. 'Leave him alone, you great hulking brute. Can't you see he's had enough?'

'I won't be through with him for a long while,' I said grimly.

I glanced down, saw him clearly for the first time, his agonised eyes, the blood that masked the lower part of his face, the blood that was dripping on him from my own cut eye.

'You can't do it,' she half-sobbed. 'You've gotta let him go. D'you hear me? You can't beat him up this way.' She was wrenching my shoulder, trying to tear me away from him.

I was staring down at him in bewilderment. Now I could see him in the light of the flashlamp, it wasn't the guy who had pumped shots at me in the cafe. It was another guy, a guy with small features, and a pert face that was vaguely familiar.

'Hank,' she pleaded. 'Don't hurt him anymore. Please don't hurt him anymore.'

I shook her away from me savagely, stared for long seconds at the guy groaning beneath me, and then looked up at Cora.

My mouth was dry. I said, hoarsely: 'What is this guy to you, anyway?'

There was a momentary hesitation before she replied, and I knew she was lying. 'He's nothing to me, Hank. I've never seen him before.'

'He's gonna get what's coming to him,' I growled. 'He's taken six shots at me tonight, and I'm going to pay him for every one.'

'You're crazy, Hank,' she sobbed hysterically. 'He'd never do that. He'd never shoot anyone. He hasn't even got a gun.'

I got up slowly, stood over him. He blinked in the sharp light of the flashlight, drew the back of his hand across his puffed and bleeding lips.

I said, menacingly: 'You stay just right where you are. One move out of you, and you're gonna get it.'

He looked up at me apprehensively, and I knew he was beat, all the fight knocked out of him.

She said, piteously: 'It wasn't him that shot at you, Hank. He hasn't even got a gun.'

I grasped her arm, snarled my fingers deep into flesh. 'Who is he?' I demanded hoarsely. 'What do you know about him?'

'I … he …' She broke off, took a deep breath, and when she spoke again, there was pleading and anxiety in her voice. 'Do trust me, Hank. He didn't try to shoot you. Let him go, will you?'

'What's he doing here?' I grated. 'What does he want?'

'Honestly, Hank. I don't know. I don't know.'

I took a deep breath. 'There's one good way to find out,' I gritted. 'A coupla hours in the sweat-room with the cops will make him loosen up.'

There was a strangled sob of protest in her voice. 'Don't hand him over to the cops, Hank. *Please* don't hand him over.'

I pulled her right up close against me, pushed my face down against hers. 'Come clean, then,' I rasped. 'Who is he? What does he want?'

'He's my brother,' she whispered, so softly I could hardly hear her.

I let the air whistle out through my lips slowly. I'd half-guessed at it, but it was still difficult to believe.

'So he's your brother,' I growled. 'So what's he doing here?'

She wailed: 'Promise you'll let him go, Hank?'

'He tried to kill me,' I said deliberately. 'Six shots.'

'But he didn't, Hank,' she protested desperately. 'He didn't. He couldn't. He wouldn't kill anyone.'

'He wouldn't kill anyone any more than you would unlock the door of Rosa Greigs' bedroom and give her an opportunity to kill herself,' I snarled.

I sensed the shocked surprise inside her, instinctively sensed it was real shock, real surprise.

'What on earth are you talking about?' she gasped.

'You know what I'm talking about,' I gritted. 'You've been making headway with old Greigs. It would break just right if she knocked herself off.'

She recoiled from me. 'You don't think I'd do a thing like that!'

'Why did you spend so long out at my car?'

She bit her lip, said nothing.

I waited.

She still said nothing.

I stirred the guy lying on the ground with my foot. 'Okay, sonny, I said. Let's get going. The cops are gonna have plenty to ask you.'

She held on to my arm. 'Please, Hank. Please don't hand him over to the police. He's never done anything wrong before.'

I drew a deep breath. 'What's little brother been doing this time, then, honey? Apart from taking a few shots at me.'

She said, piteously: 'Don't let the police get their hands on him. If we make full restitution, will you let him go? You'll get everything back.'

'And just what is everything?' I demanded.

'The Roman relics,' she said quietly, 'Philip took from the safe.'

It took me a few seconds to digest that. 'And this is your brother, Philip,' I said, stirring him with the toe of my shoe. He cowered away from me.

She nodded dumbly.

I was beginning to see what a blind fool I was. 'You were the inside man,' I accused. 'You played on the old guy, pumped the information out of him. And it worked out even better than you expected. He dropped everything into your lap.'

She nodded again. 'It was an opportunity too good to miss. I knew Philip would be around, casing the joint from outside. I slipped out to tell him how easy it would be to pull it tonight.'

'Told him where to find the alarm, told him how to open the safe.'

She nodded.

'You're copper-bait,' I snarled. 'You're both pleading for a long ride down the river. How could a couple of extra smart kids like you be so dumb? Don't you know you can't shift that stuff, that every collector in the country will know about it?'

She said quietly, dully: 'There are plenty of collectors who would pay and say nothing; be content to have those pieces in their possession.'

Philip spoke for the first time. 'It's no good, sis,' he said despairingly. 'I tried, but we didn't make it. We've just gotta take the consequences.' He was an abject figure now, forlorn and bloodied.

She said, piteously: 'Philip isn't to blame. It was my idea. He didn't want to have anything to do with it. But I talked him into it. If you wanna inform the cops, can't you let Phil go. I'll admit to everything, admit I did it by myself.'

I took the torch from her hand, shone it on her face.

She was sincere, meant every word she said. I swung the torch down and around on to Philip. I said harshly. 'Where d'ya put the stuff?'

He jerked his head. 'Buried beneath the tree over there.'

'Show me,' I ordered. 'And don't get up. Crawl on hands and knees.'

I kept a firm grip on Cora's arm as we followed him. At the base of a pine tree, he'd scraped cones and twigs together to cover the shallow hole he'd dug. They were all there, snugly wrapped in cotton wool. My fingers were gripping Cora's arm so tightly it musta bruised her. I said: 'Are you on the level about taking the rap for this jerk?'

She dropped her eyes. 'Yes,' she said dully. 'Let him go. I'll take the blame. And it's just. Because he didn't want to do it. I made him.'

I looked at Philip as he groped around on all fours, peering up at me through the bright glare of the flashlamp. 'You hear what your sister says, kid? Is that the way you want it?'

'We're both in it together,' he said obstinately.

'Philip,' she said quietly. 'I promised Mother. This means a chance for you. I promised Mother I'd look after you. Are you going to go?'

'I can't leave you, sis,' he protested.

'You've got to,' she said desperately. 'Can't you see, it's the only way.'

There was a long silence.

'What about it, kid?' I demanded. 'Are you gonna beat it, or are you gonna string along with your sister to face the cops?'

He hovered uncertainly.

She stamped her foot in sudden annoyance. 'It's a chance in a thousand, Philip. You've got to take it. D'you hear me. You've got to take it.'

He looked from her to me uncertainly.

'On your feet, kid,' I growled. 'Scram. Scram while the going's good.'

He climbed to his feet, stood staring uncertainly.

'Philip,' she said, with exasperation. 'For God's sake!'

There was a kinda choked sob in his voice as he turned away, shambled off into the darkness.

I stood there waiting for several minutes. Then Cora said, with that dull note in her voice: 'All right, Hank. I'm ready.'

I shone the torch down on the relics. 'These have got to be returned,' I said. 'Make an apron of your dress, put them in that.'

She stooped down, spread her dress across her slim thighs, carefully deposited the relics in the apron, and stood up again, waiting for my next order.

'We're taking them back to the house,' I said grimly.

We walked there side by side, Cora numbed and silent, inwardly tormented.

When we got near the house, I asked: 'Were you on the level

about not opening Mrs Greigs' bedroom?'

'Yes,' she said dully. 'I couldn't marry Greig if he had all the money in the world.'

'When d'you find that out?'

'While I was softening him up,' she sighed. 'Each time he touched me, I got cold shivers down my spine.' She shuddered. 'Folks have all kinds of good intentions, think out plans logically and intelligently, and then suddenly they discover they've got emotions, that they're human and that their brain and body have got to live in harmony.'

'I've been thinking things over, too,' I said bitterly. 'This'll be your first conviction?'

'Yes,' she said numbly, bleakly.

I rubbed it in a little more. 'You're gonna find it tough getting a job when you come out.'

She bit her lip, said nothing.

'You're a crazy dame,' I said. 'Your trouble is that you're maladjusted. Why don't you get yourself a job? You're smart enough, intelligent enough to go places. Maybe you might meet somebody you really like.'

She burst out angrily: 'Hell. What I've got coming to me is bad enough. You don't have to preach as well, do you?'

'I just wanna be sure you know the kinda mess you've landed yourself in. And why!'

'You don't have to tell me,' she snarled. 'I can add two and two.'

We were near the house now. I said: 'Leave the talking to me. Understand?'

She said, resentfully: 'I suppose I ought to thank you for letting Philip go free.'

'Thank yourself. You put up arguments he never could have put up.'

She said quickly: 'And you really won't breathe a word about him. You really will give him a break?'

'You figure he knows how to use it?'

'I guess so. He would have been a good kid, if it hadn't been for me.'

'What's stopping you from being a good kid?'

'I guess I learned too late.'

The others were just gathering at the steps of the house as we got within range. I shouted to them and they came hurrying over.

'I've got them,' I said. 'You haven't anything to worry about.'

Greigs was panting, nearly fainted with relief. 'They're all right?' he asked. 'There's nothing missing? Nothing broken?'

'I don't think so,' I told him. 'They've been handled with care.'

Anderson demanded: 'Where is the thief? What happened to him?'

I took a deep breath, said slowly: 'I found him trying to hide them in a hole he had made. I surprised him, but he got away. I tripped over a root and cut my eye. Otherwise I'd have caught him.'

Anderson said alertly: 'Maybe he's still around somewhere.'

'I don't think so,' I replied quickly. 'I was dazed for a few minutes. He's had plenty of time to have got clear.'

'Did you see him, Cora?' asked Anderson.

She looked at me meaningfully. 'No,' she said shortly.

Greigs was fussing around the relics in Cora's skirt like an old hen around her chicks. 'Get them into the house and check that they're all safe,' he urged.

I looked at Cora meaningfully, took a deep breath. 'He was a smart guy,' I said. 'He had everything figured out. It was just sheer bad luck he didn't get away with it. And our good luck.' I took another deep breath, flashed Cora another warning glance. 'Guys who work single-handed like that are always the smartest.'

Cora's eyes were wide with mystification. No-one seemed to notice her expression, because they were climbing the steps to the house now, Greigs taking the lead, guiding Cora carefully by the arm to make sure she didn't trip and spill the contents of her apron onto the floor.

Greigs led the way straight through to the ground floor

dining room and over to the table, where he spaced out the relics carefully with trembling fingers.

I caught Sheila's eye. She was standing beside Rosa Greigs, who was seated in a chair, looking very frail and wan, her eyes closed and her hands knotted in her lap.

I crossed over to Sheila. 'How is she?'

'She's all right now,' she told me. 'A little reaction at first, but she's recovered now.' She glanced across at Greigs. 'Look at that old coot,' she sneered. 'So tied up with ancient history he's forgotten about his wife.'

I bent down, stared into Mrs Greigs' face. 'Hello,' I said smilingly. 'Remember me?'

She stared at me. She said in a terse, harsh voice. 'Yes. I remember you. You pulled me out of the river.'

'You must be very unhappy,' I said.

'I am,' she told me. 'I don't want to live.' Tears welled in the corners of her eyes and glistened on her eyelashes. 'I don't want to live,' she said tearfully. 'I want to die. Why won't they let me die?'

'It's because you're not well you feel like this,' I said quietly. 'You're almost better now. But you're depressed and unhappy. The doctors say you're nearly better, but you've got to do what the doctors say.'

Tony Gilmore, her brother, loomed up alongside me. He'd poured himself another brandy, was cuddling it like a long-lost brother.

Rosa Greigs wailed: 'No-one wants to help me. Warren is the only one who wants to help me. And then all of you stopped me tonight.'

I looked up slowly at Sheila. She was staring at me. I said, quietly: 'What do you mean, Mrs Greigs? Why does Warren want to help you?'

'He knows I don't want to live,' she sobbed. 'But Warren is good to me. He opened the door for me. H» doesn't think I know, but I saw him do it. He's the only one who's trying to help me.'

I straightened up. But I was slow off the mark. Tony was

already halfway across to Anderson, and an amazing change had come over him. He was no longer happy and contented. Instead, he was forceful and vigorous.

He grasped Anderson by the shoulder, swung him around and gave him the neatest uppercut I've ever seen.

Anderson traversed the room backwards on his heels, tripped on the carpet and sat down hard. There was blood streaming from his nostrils, and a dazed look in his eyes as he groped frantically for his horn-rimmed glasses.

Cora stared, Greigs stared, the butler stared.

With an uncanny swiftness, Tony stooped over Anderson, dragged him to his feet, hammered another pile-driver dead centre of Anderson's pan, sending him crashing backwards a second time.

'Tony,' cried Greigs, horrified.

'Stay out of this,' warned Tony grimly. 'I've just learned how Rosa's been getting out on her own. This guy let her out tonight.'

It made sense. Because Anderson was the guy who was gonna be the administrator of the Greigs' estate. It could suit him to have control of the finances.

Greigs didn't catch on quick. He said, 'What are you talking about, Tony? How can you say such a thing?'

'Ask your wife,' snarled Tony. 'Ask her who opened her bedroom door for her tonight.'

Anderson wasn't a fighting man, and any fight he might have had in him had been knocked out by those first two pile-drivers. Tony dragged him to his feet, smashed him down a third, fourth and fifth time.

There was nobody to stop Tony except me. And the way I figured it, a beating was the only thing that could be pinned on Anderson. You can't stick a guy in jail merely for opening a locked bedroom door.

Deliberately I turned my shoulders, left Tony to finish the job he was executing quite nicely.

Greigs came running over to me, seized my arm. 'You've got to stop him,' he pleaded. 'Tony s gone crazy or something.'

'Ask your wife why Anderson's good to her.'

He looked at me, looked down at his wife. 'Is Warren good to you, my dear?'

She looked at him, looked at me. She said fiercely: 'You're no good, none of you. I want to die and you won't let me. Warren is the only one who'll help me, and now you're punishing him.'

'How can Warren help you, my dear?' he asked, in a quavering voice.

'He let me out of my room,' she said.

Cora was looking at me appealingly. She was still wondering why I had given her a chance. She said abruptly, like she couldn't believe it: 'Do you really mean it, Hank?'

I eyed her steadily. 'Once in a while, everyone gets a break. The only thing I can hope is that you don't make the same mistake a second time.'

Her eyes were shining gratefully. 'I won't make the same mistake again,' she said sincerely.

Sheila was watching me, shrewdly. I didn't like to think what she was making of our conversation.

'Well, thanks for everything,' said Cora quietly.

Sheila said quietly: 'You've got to stop him, Hank. He'll beat him to death.'

I managed to stop Tony with some difficulty. Anderson was quite cold by this time, had received a thrashing he wouldn't ever forget. His face was a red smear. But a broken nose and mouthful of smashed teeth was a cheap get out for Anderson.

Tony said, through his teeth: 'Help me get him out of this house. If he ever dares to come again, I'll kill him.'

He picked up Anderson like he was a sack of potatoes, hoisted him over his shoulder, made for the front door. I followed him, scared he might throw him down the steps. Not that Anderson didn't deserve it. But I didn't want to see Tony on a homicide charge. Anderson had the look of a guy whose skull cracks easily.

Tony knew where he was going. He walked down the front steps, set off across the lawn. It wasn't until we got to it that I realised what he had in mind.

It was a goldfish pond. Wide, and maybe a foot deep, with a thick layer of mud at the bottom. Tony deposited Anderson so carefully, he didn't even recover consciousness as the cold water lapped up over his waist, his head lolling against the stone flagging that surrounded the pond.

'He might slip,' I warned. 'His head might go under the water.'

'That's a risk I'm willing to take,' gritted Tony, and he took my arm finally, urged me back towards the house.

There were a lot of things to be done. We had to phone for a doctor to examine Rosa Greigs, and the garage to remove the cars sardined together in the drive gates. Finally we debated if we should telephone the police and report the robbery of the antiques.

I was all against it, for obvious reasons, Tony was disinterested, Sheila was silent and Greigs was strongly opposed to publicity of any kind.

We agreed we would keep the police out of it, since we'd recovered all we'd lost without breakage.

I looked at Cora, looked at Sheila. 'How about it, kids?' I said. 'It's getting late. We've had as much excitement as we can take for one evening. Time for bed now.'

Greigs said: 'What about your car?'

'That's okay,' I said airily, but feeling sick again. 'The insurance company will take care of it. We can get a taxi back from here.'

'It seems I'm always indebted to you, Mr Janson. If there's anything I can do at any time ...'

'Forget it,' I said. 'Things like this happen. But there is one thing you can do. Phone for a cab.'

We had to scramble over the two crushed cars to get out to the taxi. I sat in the middle between both of them, and there wasn't a thing to say.

Cora slipped her hand down alongside me, caught my fingers in hers, squeezed my hand gratefully.

'Thanks for everything,' she whispered, and her perfume was as subtle and as tantalising as I always remembered it.

We drove to Cora's flat first. I got out of the cab, held the door for her, helped her down. She looked at Sheila, looked at me, said in a small, controlled voice: 'If you'd like coffee, Hank, I'd be pleased to make you some.'

I could sense Sheila in the semi-gloom of the cab, watching me with green eyes that glowed with anger. I said uncomfortably: 'It's okay, kid. I guess it's late. We'd better be getting along.'

She said softly: 'I really am grateful for everything, Hank. And if there's anything you want, look me up, Hank. I'll always be pleased to see you.'

'Sure, kid,' I said. 'Sure.'

There was icy silence in the cab when we got moving again. I moved closer to Sheila, she moved away from me, I moved closer still. She pressed herself tight up against the corner of the cab.

I gave up.

But I didn't give up. Because this row between Sheila and me had been going on too long. Moreover, Sheila was the kinda dame I go for.

When we reached her apartment block, I dismissed the taxi-driver, paid him off and followed her upstairs to her apartment. She paused outside with the key in her hand. 'I'm not issuing invitations to coffee,' she said bitingly.

'You make such nice coffee.'

'Scram, you louse,' she said, in a cold, biting voice. 'Of all the two-timing, double-crossing, cheap tin jacks, you're about the worst. Now scram, will ya? Before I'm ill.'

'Listen, Sheila,' I pleaded. 'That dame doesn't mean a thing to me. I don't know how I can convince you, but ...'

She'd opened up the door, pushed her way inside.

I tried to follow her, got my hand around the door. She musta been burning with anger, because she slammed the door with an almost incredible strength.

I howled with the pain of my crushed fingers, and she opened the door just enough for me to draw my hand clear. Then she slammed the door again, leaving me nursing bruised and bleeding fingers, snarling with the agony of them.

The things a dame can do to a guy!

It was some minutes before the initial pain died away and I could breathe freely. I glared balefully at Sheila's door, decided against breaking through it to give her the hiding of her life, and walked slowly back along the corridor and down the stairs to the entrance hall.

I hadn't had a pleasant evening. I'd been punched, pummelled, kicked and shot at. I'd been compelled to smash my own car, spent half the evening chasing through woods, getting my face and legs torn and scratched. I'd been shot at and nagged at, and finally I'd had my hand crushed.

I wasn't feeling happy.

I was feeling savage.

Very savage!

I walked down the apartment steps, paused for a moment to light a cigarette, and then with black, sullen hatred for all mankind simmering inside me, I started walking home.

I have my moods. This was one of the foulest and blackest moods I'd had for a long time. It was one of those moods that needs just one more straw to snap the last thread of self-control.

And the last straw was added.

It came out of the darkness from across the road, a spurt of flame and the soft plop of a silencer. Just once more I was lucky. The bullet sang through the air not an inch from my ear.

And that was it!

I went berserk.

I forgot sanity and forgot fear. I forgot everything except that there was someone I hated within reach on whom I could vent all my anger.

If I hadn't have been so mad, I wouldn't have been successful. Because by all natural laws I should been killed. He shoulda plugged me again and again as I stormed blindly towards him, jet-propelled by blind, killing rage.

Maybe the very unexpectedness and craziness of my attack upset him. He didn't try to escape. He just stood there and shot at me as I rushed straight at him, hearing the silencer spit twice more and hearing lead ricochet on the buildings behind me.

He never got the chance to fire a fourth time. I hit him with the impact of a shell, smashed into him, slammed him clean off his feet with the battering impact of my body.

Then I was like a mad beast, smashing and pounding, twisting, kneading and tearing. There was a roar in my ears that was strangely mingled with hoarse breathing, the sound of opening windows, slamming doors and loud, shouting voices.

There were hands grasping me, pulling me away from him, and I was fighting them all, fighting to get my hands around that killer who was the symbol of my frustrated anger.

The voices were urgent and anxious. Somebody shouted, 'He's killing him,' and then the hands were too numerous to resist, were bearing me over backwards, crushing me down, suffocating me, grinding the wind from my body.

The crushing weight was there for an eternity. Mingled with it was the sound of cop sirens and authoritative official voices, the lessening of the weight that cramped my chest, and like a sweet bell ringing across the countryside, Sheila's voice pleading tearfully: 'Have they hurt you, Hank? Have they hurt you?'

She came back from the kitchen with another ice-bag, changed it for the one I was wearing. I looked at her through the one eye that wasn't closed, worked up a grin.

'Quite a nurse, aren't you, Scallywag?'

Her face was white and set. 'You had me scared, Hank,' she said faintly. 'They said there'd been shooting, and I thought you'd been killed.'

'Not this time,' I chuckled.

'Keep still,' she ordered.

I was stripped to the waist. She bent down, applied alcohol once more to the ugly weal searing along my side. As I winced with the sting of it, she said: 'A few inches to the left, and that bullet would have made a stiff of you.'

She was bending over me, quite close. She looked prettier

than I remembered seeing her before. I reached out, touched the hair at the back of her neck. She didn't pull away. I saw a flush mount to her cheeks.

'You're not really mad at me, Scallywag,' I asked softly. 'It's true about that dame, there isn't anything between us.'

She said quietly: 'Why did he do it, Hank? Why did he want to kill you?'

'Aw, the guy was crazy!'

'Why did he want to kill you?' she persisted.

'You heard what the cops said. They've got him taped. Knew all about him.'

'Why was he gunning for you? Why was he so set on killing you?'

I took a deep breath. 'Remember Lawson? Earl Lawson?'

'Sure I remember. That Argentine white slave trafficker you exposed a coupla years ago.'

'He got a life sentence,' I told her.

'I remember reading about it.' She grinned wryly. 'I do read the *Chicago Chronicle* at times.'

'That's the reason,' I said.

She puckered her forehead. 'I don't get it.'

'This guy's Lawson's brother,' I explained. 'He was in jail when Lawson arrived there. Lawson made him promise to get me.' I sighed. 'He sure did his best.'

I saw her eyelashes were shiny with tears. 'Gee, kid,' I said. 'What's biting you?'

'Take care of yourself, Hank,' she whispered, and suddenly she was sobbing.

I put my arm around her, and her head quite naturally rested against my chest. I patted her shoulder. 'You've got nothing to worry about, kid,' I said.

'I just don't want anything to happen to you,' she sobbed.

'I tell you what, Scallywag,' I said brightly, like I'd just hit on a bright idea. 'I'll stay here tonight. Then you'll know for sure I'm not getting into any trouble.'

Other Crime Titles available from Telos Publishing

MIKE RIPLEY
JUST ANOTHER ANGEL
ANGEL TOUCH
ANGEL HUNT
ANGELS IN ARMS
ANGEL CITY
ANGEL CONFIDENTIAL
FAMILY OF ANGELS
THAT ANGEL LOOK
BOOTLEGGED ANGEL
LIGHTS, CAMERA, ANGEL
ANGEL UNDERGROUND
ANGEL ON THE INSIDE
ANGEL IN THE HOUSE
ANGELS AND OTHERS

ANDREW HOOK
THE IMMORTALISTS
CHURCH OF WIRE

ANDREW PUCKETT
DESOLATION POINT
BLOODHOUND
SHADOWS BEHIND A SCREEN

EVGENY GRIDNEFF
A STINK IN THE TALE

TANITH LEE
DEATH OF THE DAY

www.ingramcontent.com/pod-product-compliance
Lightning Source LLC
Chambersburg PA
CBHW071829190726
48292CB00005B/1689